Short Lived

A selection of short stories for the everyday.

By Jenny Lippmann and Victoria Hunter

Contents

Mr Clarence's Hot Chocolate Varieties

Just focus on the coffee; things can only get better...

The main road has been gritted, but the narrow pavements here are ankle-deep in sugar-white snow. For a tempting moment, I consider sprinting down the road, shouting and waving like a bad imitation of It's a Wonderful Life. I'm so desperate for a hot drink that the endless white stretch is conjuring up steamed latte milk before my eyes.

It's been the morning from hell. For the first time in my career to date, I'm actually glad to escape the confines of the library, fully resigned to a caffeine and yoghurt lunch – mainly because I can't afford the current commercial price of a cheese toastie, but yet similarly can't stand to sit for an hour in the library staff room, where a bitter silence is festering.

I'll take hunger over Carl's mutely glaring negativity any day - and considering I just suffered through a particularly intense hour of it, the gnawing pain of my stomach eating itself right now feels almost friendly by comparison.

Don't believe me? Okay, let me recap.

'We need a winter holiday activity session for the kids.' New, young and the only librarian, I'd looked around at the group enthusiastically. 'Any ideas?'

'Get an author in?' Maggie suggested.

'Too expensive.' Carl fired back, immediately.

'Read and review contest?' Susie looked hopeful. The laser-eye shifted to her, witheringly.

'We need them to come in and read first.'

'Okay then,' I spoke up, loudly, trying to cover Susie's humiliation. 'How about –'

Carl cut me off with thirty years of well-crafted disdain. 'We must remain conscious of budget cuts. It must be suitable. And we must consider staffing levels.'

I stared around the table at all ten of us in disbelief. Sometimes, I swear, it's like he desperately wants us to fail; a bureaucratic puppet counting off the days to retirement... And he's particularly out to destroy me at the same time. I realise that sounds dramatic, but it's true - like I said, I'm new; I'm young and I'm the only officially qualified librarian of the group... Oh, and I also don't really play by the very-tightly-restrictive rules.

Yeah, that may have something to do with it.

But the way I see it, we need people to come in and keep our library open at any cost. So we need to keep up with the times; sadly Carl and his fellow managerial bureaucrats are practically coated with dust as they slump in their office chairs, scared to even speak to a member of the public in case it means they have to actually do their jobs.

And yes, I realise how harsh that sounds, but trust me, you have to see this level of insane bureaucracy to believe it. Add to that the fact that, despite my best efforts, any attempt on my part to do my own job and draw people into the library keeps being shot down in a burst of violent flame, you can see why I've become so caffeine dependent. It's exhausting having ridiculous, non-existent flaws picked on in all your innovative ideas - not to mention thoroughly depressing, because at the end of it all, if I don't get people to come in, it's my head that will be rolling...

Unfair? Yes. Hence my irritation at the aforementioned dire staff meeting, where yet another soul-destroying, idea-bashing humiliation was taking place.

'Perhaps we could do something science-based? That's very popular at the moment - Brian Cox and all that?' Isobel caught my eye rather than Carl's, which I appreciated; it was a good idea, I could already see ways we could run with it...

'Absolutely, that would be brilliant. We could use bits of scrap coloured paper and all that glitter lying around from the summer, get the kids to make our own display of the solar system to go up on the boards...'

'Yeah,' Isobel agreed, picking up the pace, 'The Sun right through to Pluto!'

'Isobel,' Carl's tone was withering - the cringing crash-and-burn moment was imminent. 'Pluto is not a planet.'

When the metaphorical bell rang, I fled.

It can only get better – come what may, you still have your love of books – and chocolate...
And caffeine.

Kicking my way through flurried drifts, I'm finally at the coffee shop and its solid warmth greets me like a long-lost friend; my winter triumvirate of hat, scarf and mittens will soon be abandoned, replaced with the glowing, bitter kick of beautiful, steaming coffee... I step towards the counter –

And realise that there's something wrong. There's barely more than two people in here. Anywhere else, on a snowy, almost Arctic day, that might be normal. But here there's only one high street coffee shop and I'm standing in it. Jeff Wayne's Musical War of the Worlds could be happening outside, Martians blasting houses and Richard Burton rumbling in the background – the locals would still be crammed in here, queuing for their lattes.

The teenager behind the counter is as twitchy as a cornered gazelle.

'Cappuccino please?'

'I'm-sorry-but-the-coffee-machine-is-completely-broken-today,' He bursts it out in one breath and steps back. I wonder how many other pent-up caffeine dependents have railed at him so far today. Not that I want to rail at him. No, I just want to crawl across the counter and bawl into his shoulder how much I need a warm, artificially stimulated drink to help ease my defeat and nurse my courage. I'll even eat the beans raw if I have to.

Somehow, though, I manage to restrain myself.

7

'Sounds like your morning has been as good as mine.' I muster up a reassuring smile; not just for his benefit, but my own too. I need to make sure Carl hasn't destroyed it.

'We can still do smoothies,' He offers. I don't need to raise a sceptical eyebrow towards the sub-zero temperatures outside the window for him to see how inappropriate this suggestion is. He rapidly clears his throat. 'Or hot chocolate?'

I hesitate.

It's a universal paradox that, unless you have a fantastic cafetière, coffee is usually better when someone else prepares it for you – yet with hot chocolate, the opposite applies. Bitter cocoa, stove-warmed milk, a couple of marshmallows... None of this over-sweetened, whipped-cream, commercial nonsense.

But I'm cold, tired and grateful to be out.

Five minutes later, I'm languishing at one end of a booth, a steaming frothy mug warming my palms. I've fished my notebook out of my bag, determined to devise a kids' holiday activity that Carl can't possibly object to – book-related, yet wintery, with the potential for active creativity - no cost, no extravagant staffing requirements, no politically disputable planets...

Oh good God, I'm done for.

My guardian angel must be on strike.

I take a consoling sip of hot chocolate; the warmth of it pierces my tongue, a rippling, tangy, creamy delectation that flushes my cheeks instantly. I can't stop myself wincing at the first burst of sweetness in the aftertaste though.

'Not enough cocoa these days, right?'

The voice comes from the other end of the booth – an older man, taking a break from his newspaper to watch me. Probably wondering at a fellow stalwart's motivation to brave the freezing weather for something that isn't even caffeinated. I smile and shrug: the accepted British response.

'You know, its original popularity as a drink was precisely because there was no sugar involved.' I raise an eyebrow at his persistence, but he's beaming at me, nodding affirmatively. 'The Mayans even used chillies to add more tang!'

Another smile is rigid on my lips - but his enthusiasm is slightly infectious. If he were younger, I'd be flattered at the conversation; it'd be like one of those 'meet-cutes' in the movies. Sadly for me, he's at least three times my age – albeit kind-eyed and distinguished.

'Oh, are you a historian?'

Just can't help myself, can I? As if I don't already live enough lunches in mortal dread of one of the many library stalkers accosting me... Another universal paradox, the curse of the public servant: you can never lose face in front of anyone.

The man beams another amused smile at my question; there's something slightly knowing flickering beneath that grin.

'I guess I'm more a humanitarian. Or just Earnest. Earnest Clarence. No,' He continues, 'hot chocolate has never been the same since the introduction of the sugar base. You know, Jane Austen's contemporaries would have sipped it at breakfast each morning; no wonder they wore dresses with no waistlines.'

He winks at me jovially and, surprisingly, I'm smiling back.

'But of course, the bitterness is the real joy of the drink – a creamy flood that lingers at the back of the throat, with an aftertaste to make your cheeks curl. Like Edmund Pevensie drank. As I'm sure you know, C. S. Lewis spent many iced winters like this in Oxford.' He gestured vaguely at the window. 'What better drink for frozen Narnia? And so Edmund is served hot chocolate and – '

'Turkish Delight,' I finish. Mr Clarence has certainly piqued my interest, even if the prolonged conversation is slightly surreal. I begin to wonder if he's recognised me from the library, hence the literary-themed references.

Or perhaps he just really loves hot chocolate.

His crinkled eyes fall on my notebook. I'm something of a doodler when bored, or frustrated; I decorated this myself a couple of weeks ago, after a particularly irritating session trying to convince Carl of the success we could achieve by booking a guest speaker on F. Scott Fitzgerald. (Guess how that one worked out?) It's covered with sketches of Matilda, the BFG, Charlie...

Seeing Charlie now, clutching his golden ticket, Clarence's whole expression lights up.

'A Roald Dahl fan! You know, he really knew about chocolate. He grew up beside a chocolate factory, just like the Buckets.'

Okay – interesting, but enough now. This is growing beyond odd and a lunch break is, well, a break. I'm happy to talk about books at work; in fact, it's my favourite thing. But, nice as he seems, there's a time and a place - and it's not now. Plus there's still the riddle of the winter activity to solve...

If I'm forced into failing on this one, checkmated by Carl's stubborn bureaucracy, my job is really going to begin to suffer.

So I pointedly pull my notebook towards me, and Mr Clarence seems to get the message. As I pick up my pen and reach for my unsuspectingly-controversial drink, though, I can't help but catch his final remark, full of velvety warmth and rich as the chocolate brimming my lips.

'Dahl understood the potential of chocolate, you know – because if there's one thing kids know better than books, it's their chocolate.'

I almost drop my mug as his words register fully.

Of course!

It's perfect! This stranger's anecdotes have handed me everything I need on a silver platter – how did I not see it before? Suddenly, forgetting everything else, my notebook is open and I'm scribbling wildly, ideas seeping through my bones.

A completely chocolate themed event! Because what more do you want at Christmas, but chocolate and warmth and all the childlike excitement for the snow outside that comes with it... I could find more literary hot cocoa anecdotes, like Mr Clarence's; we could read extracts about Willy Wonka's factory - no cost there: we have the book, we're a flipping library! We could create our own chocolate waterfall for the display boards with discarded wrappers - again, no cost there; maybe even get the kids to invent their own hot chocolate recipe - all they'd need is a pen and paper...

Oh yes. I defy Carl to find fault with this one – cheap, bookish, fun... My pen trips over itself in excitement.

With every sweet, sweet sip of my drink, more ideas bubble.

Then the door clatters and I jerk upright, snapping back to reality.

Earnest Clarence is gone from the booth – and I suddenly realise I never thanked him.

Thanked him? For what, I rationalise. He couldn't have planned it, known what I needed – it was just a coincidence, the coffee machine breaking, me sitting beside a friendly chocolate fanatic...

Surely?

I consider running after him – then rationalise again. Sprinting down the road through snowdrifts, yelling thanks to Clarence? I've been watching too many movies, reading too many books. This isn't *It's A Wonderful Life*...

But as I contemplate my steaming hot chocolate, well…

I can't help but wonder.

It's Just the House Settling

'You forgot my ski poles.'

Boxes and boxes of memories surrounded them: overflowing with books or photo albums, bears that held too much sentimental value to be thrown, lamps with lopsided shades, chipped mugs, knick knacks...

Sarah scowled at him over the top of her steaming mug of tea, perched daintily on a less than dainty box marked 'SHOES'.

Brian shot her a look in return.

'We haven't been skiing for years,' he sipped at his tea wantonly and allowed a knowing grin to tug at the corners of his mouth. 'You sprained your ankle on the beginner's slope, remember? I spent the rest of the honeymoon nursing you with foot rubs and cups of hot chocolate.'

Sarah's scowl softened, and she disguised her smile by angling her head so that a curtain of blond hair swept down.

She looked around at the chaos surrounding them. 'We've got the boxes in, now it's emptying them.'

The first wave of unpacking was a blur of complaints and bickering. The arranging of bathroom mats and shampoos came with 'we had more space in the old house'. Setting out the kitchen table and all its chairs were met with 'You were supposed to fix the leg on this one.' Pushing the bed into place evoked complaints about its decorative pillows.

The brief brightness of the honeymoon memory faded, and soon, even a cup of tea wasn't enough. Sarah and Brian lay down at nine pm, tuckered out from their day of travelling, of moving to the modern house on the hip edge of the city. Brian set his alarm for an early start, and rolled onto his side.

Sarah sighed audibly, staring at the glass of water on her bedside table. She couldn't close her eyes; new house, and all that.

There was a beat.

The water shuddered.

Sarah shifted, frowning slightly. It could have been a trick of the light, or the way the moon beams fell through the windows.

'Just the house settling,' Brian muttered, sensing her anxiety. Sarah nodded and closed her eyes, settling into a restless sleep.

The next evening, amongst the clutter, Brian spied a box of 'old' photographs forgotten and bent, always put aside for albums that had yet to be bought. He took up a handful and looked at photo after photo, mostly from the wedding. That first dance to the cheesy title track to 'Mannequin', taken straight out of the eighties and dropped haphazardly into a wedding in 2010. Sarah had grinned all over her face, having let Brian choose the music because she loved him that much. They'd swayed and held one another – even as the heel of Sarah's shoe

15

snapped and sent her careering forward. Brian had of course caught her, managing to pass it off as a romantic dip.

They didn't smile like that nearly as often as they should.

Brian made the decision to temporarily place the photos in the basement – because they would see them again, wouldn't they? – And he abandoned them there without word, pulling at his collar as he left the oddly humid basement to return upstairs.

They had finally managed to move in a sofa, where Sarah had already planted herself. Brian took a place at the other end, the two of them distanced, still sitting in a war zone of random items kicked up by the whirl wind of the move. The ski poles almost pointedly lay in the middle of the floor, amongst the clutter.

Watching a television programme proved a difficulty, fifteen minutes in. Soaps were matched with 'Olympic Football' and in between that, 'necessary' trips to the gym were implied, along with a snide mention of 'that bloke' Sarah worked with who was supposedly 'giving her the eye'.

'And anyway,' Brian pouted. 'It's not like he has to deal with your insufferable friends.'

It went on like this throughout a BBC documentary about volcanos, until the sofa rocked – the sofa, and everything else within the room, and most likely the house – and an audible rumble followed, similar to that of a fairly distant growl.

Sarah and Brian looked sharply at one another.

'It's just the house settling,' Brian announced, hardly aware that he had said it at least four times in the past two days. Sarah waved a dismissive hand, a gesture that quickly turned into a frantic one.

'What if it's the boiler?'

'It's nowhere near the boiler, it's coming from the basement and anyway, we haven't been down there yet, have we?'

Sarah blanched and leapt to her feet, taking up one of her ski poles from the living room floor.

'You're arming yourself? You're seriously arming yourself?' Brian raised his eyebrows and followed, picking up the other ski pole, feeling rather idiotic. 'At least these'll be used for something.' He smirked, following his wife down into the cellar. She ignored him and switched the light on.

The bulb came to life, lighting the dingy room. The walls were made up of exposed brick, like a game of completed Tetris, and the only remaining things down there were a steel bed frame, a collection of newspapers from the 1970's and the box of photos that still needed arranging. Sarah looked around bravely, and lowered her pole. 'Perhaps it was the pipes. Maybe we should call a plumber.'

Brian didn't reply. He had found a loose brick in the flooring. He looked towards Sarah.

'Love, come look at this.' He moved the brick away, and then another, followed by another. Sarah crouched over him, frowning as he pulled more and more of the floor away. 'That's bad, that,' he said with disapproval, removing so many now that the pair of them had to back up. Beneath, a wooden trap door was gradually being revealed.

Once the handle came into view, Sarah swapped a look with her husband and took hold of it, pulling hard. The hatch shrieked - the hinges rusted with age – and another violent rumble shook them, sending them stumbling into one another. A hot gust of air followed, and Brian pulled out his phone, using the built in light to shine on the contents within.

They peered in together. The space beneath the house was enormous, and of tremendous depth. Something twitched in the shadows and Sarah flinched while Brian waved a dismissive hand.

'It's just the house-'

'Brian, for God's sake, it's not the bloody house settling. There's a dragon living down there!' Sarah brandished her ski pole in the general direction of the hatch, and when Brian craned his neck to get a look in, he was surprised to find that there was, in fact, a dragon beneath their house.

The light of the mobile phone illuminated row upon row of green scales. They flashed and glinted, and as Brian angled the light further in, a globe sized eye caught it; open wide and angry. A tail flicked back and forth in the darkness, displaying one long row of spines along it, like grave stones in an emerald cemetery. Sarah fumbled to use her own phone to bring attention onto it. The dragon made no noise and it did not twitch. It simply watched and waited.

Brian straightened up, rubbing his head. 'The estate agent didn't mention this. Should I give him a ring?'

Sarah crouched down on her haunches, noting the wide passageway tunnelling out, obviously spanning much further than the foundations of just their house and even the street.

'It's not trapped down there at any rate. Maybe call Pest Control? The estate agents won't know what to do with the thing…'

*

'That's a type forty-two you've got there,' said the pest control officer, peering into the hole with his industrial torch. It illuminated far more of the dragon than the mobile phone did – drawing particular attention to the spines on its back and its twitching ears; it's movements were almost robotic in the gloom, and each scale gleamed like tin foil in the torchlight. Sarah and Brian watched on with anxious frowns. The man got to his feet. 'Domestic dragon. Typically found in the underground of Suburbia. They feed on a certain atmosphere,' he gestured to the wisps of smoke rising up out of the exposed hatch. 'This one's enjoying itself.'

'Well, what do you suggest?' Asked Sarah. 'When it moves in and out of its tunnel, the entire house rumbles. We can't live with that.'

'I can't make a recommendation based on the negative atmosphere of the house – that's more of a therapist's area – but I can say I can't get rid of it. Not this type, anyway.' He put his torch away in his case, shutting it with a snap. 'Good luck,' he grinned, before heading up the stairs.

What could the pest control man have meant? Brian and Sarah weren't about to admit that they had a problem.

The dragon was the problem.

With Brian and Sarah's unwillingness to change; the dragon became a regular fixture, but also a suitable distraction.

'Why didn't you tell me you didn't like my spaghetti bolognaise?' Sarah demanded one night, having caught Brian, sitting by the hatch, dangling said spaghetti over the edge and into the dragon's chasm-like mouth. Brian had looked up at her, eyebrows raised.

'Perhaps this is my way of telling you.'

Sarah pouted, but she conceded that despite Brian's childishness perhaps she should make more of an effort to handle criticism like an adult.

'Just tell me next time.' She muttered, disappearing back upstairs; to get rid of the rest of the bolognaise she had never liked, anyway.

On another occasion, Brian appeared in the basement, searching for wood varnish, only to find Sarah dropping old wellington boots, bicycle parts and hose fixtures into the hatch. Each item was promptly incinerated by the dragon.

'Sarah, what are you-'

'I told you to clear that extra crap you brought from the last garage and dumped into the new one,' she replied with some acid. 'You didn't do it.'

'I've got a lot on my plate, love,' Brian frowned. 'Why didn't you just tell me?'

Sarah looked up at him, and her eyes flashed. 'Perhaps this is my way of telling you.'

*

Months later, Brian and Sarah were still telling themselves the house was settling. The dragon came and went as it pleased, the stress that came with moving house remained, and there came a point wherein both parties realised that it wasn't just the house settling at all, and it most certainly wasn't the dragon that was the problem.

In fact, the dragon had become all too familiar.

One am. The bedroom floor rumbled as the beast below shifted. Sarah stared up at the ceiling silently; chewing on her lip. She hadn't slept properly in months. It couldn't go on this way. The walls could no longer rock, the crockery could no longer tip out of the cabinet and smash, and certainly, the arguments could go on no longer.

The house needed to be at peace.

Silently, Sarah slid out of bed and padded across the room in bare feet and nightie. She glanced back at Brian when she reached the door, but he was still. Tucking her hair behind one ear, Sarah descended the stairs, venturing through the dark depths of the house until she arrived at the door to the basement.

She flicked the switch, the lights slowly came to life, and she went down, folding her arms and shivering against the chill.

As soon as she opened the hatch, there was a burst of warmth; there always was when they opened it. This time, however, there was an accompanying smell of burning. Sarah didn't notice at first, too busy looking around mournfully at the surrounding bricks. She wondered why they had never covered the hatch back up. Why they had left it for all to see.

She stepped closer, and something crumpled beneath her foot. She halted and picked it up, only just noticing the distinct smell of burning.

Her eyes fell onto a photograph of her on a snowy slope with those ski poles, and her breath hitched. 'No…' More and more photos drifted up from the cavernous hole to join other dead images; levitated by the warm air from the dragon's lungs. Some were more charred than others, stained at the edges and curling at the corners like ancient scrolls.

'No, no, no!' She gathered them in shaking hands as they landed at her feet, crying out. She stuffed them back into their overturned box in desperation, trying and trying to salvage memories that visibly eroded before her eyes…

The dragon huffed, sending a heavy smoke up into Sarah's face. She wafted it away with a small cough and a wave of her hand, and found, when the smoke had cleared, that Brian stood beside her.

He passed her a largely undamaged photograph; smiles on the dance floor with the sweeping white dress and sharp dickey bow. He noted the drying tears beneath Sarah's eyes but didn't draw attention to them, instead shrugging with nonchalance. 'Maybe it's not just the house settling.'

They watched one another, failing to noticed how the dragon yawned, and stretched its great legs. Scales rippled and claws flexed, and soon there was a violent rumbling, which again, Sarah and Brian paid no heed to.

As the sound retreated and eventually diminished, Sarah took Brian's arm. Together, they ventured back upstairs, Brian hefting the heavy box of memories under one arm while Sarah delicately clung to the wedding photo.

Finally, the house settled.

Lollipops from Wonderland

Dear Michael,

God, I never thought I'd be doing this – sitting here, writing to no one. They said it would help, but the only thing that could possibly help would be for you to just walk in through that door, as though nothing ever happened...

I wish I'd done something different that morning. I should have made you come back; I should have held onto you tighter, told you how much I love you and how much I need you... Instead of issuing the usual 'don't forget to pick up some milk on your way home', giving you a sideways peck on the cheek; too busy to even wave you off. I'll regret that moment for the rest of my life.

And, God, Laura – I wish she wasn't old enough to know, Michael, but at six she seems to understand it all better than I do... And it's like I've lost her too; as if when the shadows fell over you, they stripped away her beautiful buttercup face as well, and I don't know how to make it better.

I thought my heart had broken completely when they told me I'd never see you again. But it's almost as if Laura is gone too – and I've realised that there are a few shards still left intact, because I can feel them splintering inside my chest now.

Please come back, Michael. I can't live without you.

I don't know what to do.

*

The phone rang shrilly throughout the house, but creaking around in the back room Morris Woods almost didn't hear it – his hearing aid was turned down again. Things had been a bit hectic so far that week and he was trying to catch up with some light pottering; since he turned eighty-three, Morris found he couldn't really handle hectic anymore...

What was it his wife, Lily, used to tease him?

'You are old, Father William, the young man said...'

That's right. Lily and her Alice in Wonderland... She had loved that particular book her entire life; indeed, she was the only person he'd ever met who could quote 'Jabberwocky' without a single mistake. Their children had loved it when – back in those heady, younger days – she would snatch up one of their wooden swords, crying 'Beware the Jabberwock, my son!' and plunging the blunt blade into some poor ted or other, amidst shrieks of laughter. Though the children eventually lost interest in such fanciful antics, Lil never lost faith in that mad, wonderful story. Morris knew that, secretly, she had hoped to repeat those scenes one day with a brood of grandchildren, but none ever came.

Instead, there had been the illness. In her last weeks, Morris would sit and read to Lily from those same dog-eared pages, trying so hard to bring the story to life as she did. He nursed a childish longing of his own, that if he spoke the words just right, he might really transport her into Wonderland, where she could live forever amongst the characters she knew so well...

This thought was still lodged with him, as were all thoughts of Lily, when he finally managed to snatch up the phone – barely two seconds before the tinny answer-machine woman clicked on.

'Hello?'

'Hi, Dad? It's Jonathon.'

'Oh, hello son.'

'How're things?'

And so it began: the usual conversation. Morris reflected briefly how funny it was; before Lily passed, she had always answered calls from their sons – she had that rare gift of always knowing what to say, never chiding or interfering. Just... perfect. It wasn't that Morris didn't want to talk to his children; words just never seemed to fit together as well for him. He was more attuned to action – doing, being, living – even if life had slowed him down a bit now.

'I put out freesias in the front window this week; your mother always liked them around this time of year.'

'Sounds nice, Dad.' Morris could hear Jonathon moving something, the tinkle of glass loud down the line. He felt a spurt of resentment for the capricious fancies of his hearing aid – it could pick up Jonathon emptying the dishwasher seventy-five miles away, but when the phone was ringing inside his own house...

'I thought about taking some next-door too,' He continued, momentarily forgetting that Jonathon didn't know what had happened next-door; he rang once a week, but it seemed to come around so quickly that Morris lost track. Days had become indistinct without Lily.

Right on cue, Jonathon paused.

'Why next-door, Dad?'

'Oh – I thought I told you? Terrible sad it is. All that rain last Thursday – when I almost came a cropper on those slick pavements? Well, late afternoon, I hear a car pull up and it's flashing blue lights in through the blind...' Morris paused, the blue glare from the police car seared into his brain like fire from Hades. 'Her husband had a car accident – died before they reached the hospital. Poor woman.'

'God, Dad, that's awful. Is that the young couple with the little girl?'

Morris nodded sadly, a wasted action, but genuinely heartfelt.

'Alice Winsor; your mother loved it when they moved in, you know. Her favourite character come to life next-door! And she liked hearing that little girl playing in the garden, said it brightened up the neighbourhood to have a little 'un running about...' He sighed heavily, before realising that it sounded like a rebuke to his childless son; quickly he carried on. 'Now she's a young widow – gone headfirst down the rabbit hole, as your mother would say.'

'That's really awful. Poor girl.'

"Funeral's next week; Mrs Gunney mentioned it when she called round to say there'll be a collection for flowers.'

'Maddest tea party of all, huh?' Morris smiled in spite of himself. That was what they'd started calling it, during those last few weeks as they made the gut-wrenching arrangements – another Lily-ism. He and Jonathon clung to Lily's Alice sayings like drowning men to life-rafts, desperate for her spirit not to slip out of reach – the only thing they ever fully shared.

'It comes to us all in the end. I do hope she'll be alright – and that little girl. She's got such a beautiful sunny smile. Lil would have known the best thing to do to help.'

'Dad,' Jonathon's tone echoed faint sternness. 'God knows it's an awful situation for the poor woman – but it's not really your place to get involved...'

'I know,' Morris cut him short, matching his son's firmness. 'I won't interfere – I know you think I stick my nose in where it's not wanted. I just don't like to think of that young woman struggling alone. Not with the little 'un, losing her father and all upset like...'

'Dad – '

'Oh, I know, son. But if your mother was here, she'd say the same. Lily always knew what to do for people, especially when things were topsy-turvy. I guess she learnt it all from that book.' Morris paused, glancing out of the window at the curve of garden leading to the grieving house next-

28

door. As he ruminated, his eyes slid down the light-spangled panes of glass, following his thoughts, until they alighted on a vase of flowers exploding in a riot of pinkish buds atop the sill. He had bought the vase for Lily on their first anniversary – every couple of weeks, for the entirety of their marriage, she had filled it with flowers. It was a practice that Morris tried to continue – for her.

A ray of sunlight shone through the crystal and it was like she was there, whispering to him. He squared his shoulders, forgetting that his son couldn't see his conviction.

'You know, I think I will take those flowers round. That poor, poor girl...'

*

Dear Michael,

I'm sorry it's been weeks since I last wrote, it's just – I guess I'm scared... of what comes next; of facing the rest of my life without ever hearing your voice again, or seeing you push your glasses up the bridge of your nose when you're concentrating, or feeling your fingers knotted through mine as we watch Laura play in the park... Little Lolly. Most of all I'm scared of ruining everything for her.

She barely speaks, Michael. She just clings onto Willoughby Bear everyday and plays silent games in her head. I still haven't seen her smile, not since...

God, all I want is for someone to tell me what to do! Tell me how to speak to her, Michael, you could always reach her, always lasso her heart and reel her back to us without even trying, like your souls were tethered together. Please, Michael; please come back –

'Why won't he come back?'

Lolly screamed that at me, you know. Last week, just as kind old Mr Woods from next-door brought us flowers. Oh, God, Michael – it was awful... I'm certain the poor man heard my heart shear in two as she cried and screamed, wanting to know where you were, because Daddy must be somewhere, so where were you?

And I couldn't answer her, our own daughter. Right when she needed me to wave my magic wand and happily-ever-after us back together... I couldn't even move. I dropped Mr Woods' beautiful flowers on the doormat and just cried. I can't do all this without you, Michael; I can't live without you...

I don't know how to make it better, and that's what mothers are supposed to do! And I can't. It's like midnight has come and suddenly I'm not all-powerful anymore – the spell has broken with my heart. I just feel so alone. The world is pitching back and forth; I can't slow it down to think, to stop it from whisking Laura away from me...

Midnight's come alright, Michael. The clocks all stopped when you were taken away from us. But that's reality, isn't it? Sometimes little girls get lost; sometimes a rabbit-hole breaks your neck.

And sometimes princes fall from ivory towers.

*

That damned phone again – why was it always ringing, just out of reach until the last second? Morris had been busy in the kitchen, cutting the stems of the roses for Lily's vase and waiting for his tea to cool. Red roses, not white. Lil had always joked that white roses made her feel like painting them, just like Alice – paint them full of passion and love, until they turned red as jam.

Thinking of Alice reminded him of the surprise he'd gotten a couple of days ago, in the garden – and at eighty-three, Morris reflected, surprises were harder to come by. He'd gone out to enjoy the sunshine, inspect the flowers – spring was coming, borne in by smatters of early cherry-blossom drifting over the back hedge like fine confetti... Lily's favourite time of year.

The gardens of the street were unusual for a set of shabby-grand detached houses. The fences between each one reached just below shoulder level, mimicking the traditional layout of terraced houses – Lil had always joked that the architect must have been relatively new at his trade, confusing designs in his eagerness. It gave a nice, open effect though, almost as if you could hop from garden to garden and the lives inhabited there. The only downside was that it also gave Mrs Gunney far too much opportunity to busy-body. Morris had been wondering what was keeping her so occupied over these last couple of weeks; he had a suspicion that it was ghoulishly intruding upon grief-stricken Mrs Winsor...

And that was when he had heard it.

'Lily!'

A sharp, desperate shout from next-door. Morris' heart had shuddered to his mouth – had time stopped for a second? If he looked up, would he find Lily on the porch step, waiting to call him for tea, back from Wonderland?

And then the cry came again, and Morris had realised his mistake with a visceral, plunging sensation.

'Lolly!'

He hadn't really registered their presence when he'd stepped outside; but, as he finally looked up and over the fence, he saw the freshly-widowed young woman from next door, half-kneeling on a scruffy blanket, surrounded by colouring books. And, upon following her wretched gaze, Morris had glimpsed a tiny figure sprinting in through the back door, a mass of blonde curls and woolly jumper, trailing a love-battered brown bear in one hand as she disappeared in a whirl of evident emotion.

Something had told Morris that it was not just the whimsical mood of a six-year old that whipped the little girl at lightning speed back inside the house.

Alice Winsor had watched her child run from her with a frantic, hopeless slumping of the shoulders, wrapping her arms around herself as if to keep her emotions from spilling out into the wilderness of the garden. Then she had looked up suddenly, aware of being observed.

She had forced a smile and, remembering it now, Morris' conscience cracked; he recognised that smile – it was the same one he had worn every day for the last however-many years since he lost Lily.

Now, with Lil fresh on his mind yet again, he recounted the episode to Jonathon across the miles, through that damned useless machine – and his resolve to try and offer at least some comfort to the poor young woman next-door strengthened with every word.

'She apologised – apologised – for their shouting interrupting me. Me. Poor young woman's got enough on her plate without worrying what I think. Lord, she looked so upset. How do you tell your little 'un that her Daddy's never coming back?'

Jonathon's murmur of agreement was lost in the tumult of Morris' thoughts.

'They call her Lolly, you know – that little girl, Laura.' A silly nickname, I know, Alice Winsor had smiled her apologetic smile again. It had vanished in embarrassment when Morris told her how he'd mistaken it for his wife's name. 'I think she worried she'd upset me further, reminding me of Lil when she called after the little 'un.'

'You're right, Dad, it must be awful – I remember how hard it was to be told about Mum and I was a grown man. But...'

Morris wasn't listening.

Smiling gently, he had wiped the mortified sorrow from Alice's face, telling her with kindly perfect words – words he knew must have come from Lily, because he had never been so self-assured before – that it was he who was sorry. He knew all too well what it felt like to lose your true love; to stay behind and pick up the shattered pieces of the life you'd built up towards the sky together.

It must be hard for your little girl – for Laura.

Her eyes had teared and suddenly it all spilt out of her, tumbling across the garden fence into Morris' comforting presence: how Little Lolly wouldn't speak, or play, or smile...

I suggested the swing – she seemed bored of colouring and I thought... It was stupid. Michael – my husband – built the swing when we first moved in; he got up before dawn, so it'd be ready for Lolly when she woke up. He told her fairies at the bottom of the garden made it for her, so that she would feel like the new house was okay – Michael always did things like that; always created little stories, devised treats and treasure hunts to make her laugh...

'Dad? Are you listening?'

Morris found that his slippered feet had walked him towards the site of his memories, back to the kitchen sink, the roses and the window overlooking the backyard. Across the fence, away into the hazy sunset dripping shadows across the Winsor's garden, he could see the towering apple tree that stood sentry against the advancing dusk. A traditional rope swing with a grainy wooden seat hung down from one outstretched bough, swinging a little in the breeze.

34

Lily used to tell him that was the tree where Alice listened to her sister reading, daydreaming against the base of its knotted trunk about white rabbits, caterpillars, croquet... She would have loved Michael Winsor's fairy story.

But what use were daydreams now, when the tree seemed to have lost its adventure, radiating only sadness?

'Look, I know you like to fix things, Dad; it's what you're good at. But people don't always mend the same way – you really shouldn't get involved.'

Jonathon's adamant tones broke through this time, as strident as a megaphone booming across a quiet afternoon. Morris sighed heavily, turning his attention back to the kitchen and reality.

'I know, son – but your mother –'

'Mum's not here, Dad. You just have to let them grieve by themselves.'

Morris felt his jaw tighten involuntarily, remembering Alice's overwhelming sorrow and the little girl – Laura, Lolly – disappearing into the back porch like a shadow in the night, shoulders shuddering with sobs. He knew exactly how that sort of grief felt. But perhaps Jonathon was right; perhaps he was being an old fool. What good could he possibly do when that poor family's whole world had been ripped apart by a nightmare?

Reluctantly, he turned the conversation to something else.

But as Morris shifted himself away from the sink, his gaze alighted on the roses once more.

Maybe he should paint Lily some white roses next week... Paint them full of passion and love...

Lily. Alice. Lolly.

Fairies.

Stories.

And suddenly he had an idea.

*

Dear Michael,

I've tried everything now. Colouring, the park, conspiring with Willoughby Bear to make chocolate button cupcakes... But "everything" is touched by your memory and Lolly... Neither of us can bear this emptiness.

And then an amazing thing happened.

Mr Woods from next-door, who brought me the flowers that night – well, he saw us last week, trying to act normally in the garden; stupid idea really, Lolly just got upset and so did I... But then I saw Mr Woods over the fence. I thought I'd upset him too, at first – he had such a strange look on his face. But... did you know he lost his wife? She was called Lily – when I shouted Lolly, he told me he thought it was her. He said they were married for sixty years, Michael. They must have felt they'd be together forever, just like us... Does it hurt more to have all those memories? Or to have the 'what-ifs', like I do?

Perhaps that's why he understands though; he didn't try to advise me, or boost me up, like everyone else. He just nodded and listened – and then, the next day, he brought Lolly a book.

Alice in Wonderland. It's beautiful, Michael – you'd have loved it. Mr Woods said it belonged to his wife, that she read it to their children when they were Lolly's age. He handed it to Laura, very solemn, but almost twinkling at her with kindness... He told her his wife, whose name was a bit like hers, had always wanted more children to read her book. His wife liked to make up stories, play games... When he talked about her, so full of love and pride – well, she reminded me of you, Michael. I think you two would have gotten along. And this book... All these pictures of such a vibrant, incredible world, where anything can happen – some of it bad, but most of it so full of life: the one thing we lost, when we lost you...

Lolly can't stop staring at it.

She thinks that's where you've gone, Michael.

To Wonderland.

She says you're there; fighting the Jabberwocks that frighten her at night, playing croquet with the Queen and Mr Woods' wife, eating jam tarts and bread and butter and oysters and lollipops that look like roses... And she keeps asking if she can see Mr Woods again soon, because he knows about Wonderland too, this magical place that you've gone to. She says she needs to ask him a question...

It's a very important question, Mummy – it's about Daddy in Wonderland.

Perhaps I should be worried, scared... I used to think that book was mad. But she's talking to me again, Michael – telling me all your adventures in Wonderland.

And, when I listen, everything suddenly doesn't hurt as much.

*

The phone rang, the usual drill – and Morris Woods ignored it. He even contemplated removing his hearing aid to better avoid the temptation of answering it.

He did feel a little guilty; Morris knew it would be Jonathon, checking in, checking up – he was pleased that his children cared enough to keep checking. Morris had never truly realised, before these days without Lily, how infinitely, fantastically important his children really were.

And now there was another child in his mind, becoming just as valuable.

Laura – Lolly.

She was the reason he was ignoring the phone now; her – and her mother. She was the reason he had walked an extra mile across town, when he went for a fresh bunch of flowers for Lil's vase; down to the Front and along the pier, stopping at every sweet shop and taffy stand – gathering supplies.

She was the reason he had made a list – and the reason he was now sat in front of his worn-out old computer, one hand clutching the mouse for dear life, trying to comprehend the complicated workings of e-bay.

Morris wasn't a complete novice. He knew how to order shopping from Sainsbury's and how to send e-mails. And he was a whizz at playing FreeCell, garnering a game-record he was quite proud of. Before Lil became sick, they would often play Hearts together, inputting silly names from the Alice books for their simulated opponents, themselves always the King and Queen. If the computer played a hand Lil didn't like, she'd crow 'off with its head!' glibly.

After she passed, Morris found a new game, too afraid of the memories glaring from the screen to go back to Hearts, but too afraid to forget her if he abandoned the computer altogether.

So he wasn't completely technophobic... But, admittedly, e-bay was something new. He'd watched Jonathon a couple of times, mainly for the novelty of learning a different computer trick, but never really anticipating he'd need it. Everything he and Lil could ever want they could buy in town, or down at the Front, only a twenty minute walk away...

Except now his list called for a number of things that he would struggle to find even in the quirky old haberdashery and wool-shop off the main street – although he had been surprised at how easily the few charity shops in town had supplied him with a good number of hats. Tentatively clicking at what looked like the right link, Morris suppressed a smile.

Sweets, hats, e-bay...

It was probably a good thing he'd ignored the phone; he would never be able to explain to Jonathon what he was trying to do.

And all because of that little 'un next door.

She had been waiting for him, towards the end of last week – stood in the garden with her mother, Lily's precious book carefully hugged to her chest and her sidekick bear crooked in the other elbow. Morris had seen them from the window; he'd been heading out to change the bird-water – Lily had been very particular about that when spring arrived, with the nests a-building and the babies a-chirruping. She had been hoping for the arrival of a Dodo one day, Morris knew.

But he'd barely gathered up his watering can before little Laura was there at the fence, peering over – and talking.

Talking to him.

'Mr Woods?'

He had smiled at her, approaching the fence softly, as if she were a little wild animal that would easily startle. Lolly had looked back over her shoulder, seeking her mother and Alice Winsor nodded encouragingly, absently stroking those blonde, haystack curls. You could see the strong resemblance between them already, Morris reflected.

'I wanted to say thank you – for the book. It's lovely.'

'You're welcome, flower. Lily would have been pleased you like it so much.'

Again, Lolly had glanced at her mother, uncertain; the bear slid into a tight stranglehold.

40

Alice Winsor had smiled at her, then at Morris, wanting him to understand.

'It's okay, Laura, you can ask Mr Woods.' The young woman cleared her throat. 'She has a question she'd like to ask you – about... Wonderland.'

'Is that where Mrs Woods is?' The words blurted out of Lolly's mouth, her big eyes solemn and earnest. Morris found himself smiling sadly.

'Well, I think so, flower.'

'My Daddy's there too.' Laura had paused and Morris remained silent; he could tell something was coming, something big – something her mother didn't know either, waiting anxiously with him for the revelation. 'Mr Woods... Do they have lollipops in Wonderland? Real lollies – like me?'

The mouse hovered over the item he wanted, the cursor trembling a little as Morris tried to collect himself, his memories, his emotions. He hadn't known how to answer the little thing, nor her mother; her question was so unutterably heart-breaking. Words had failed him – he wondered if they might have even failed Lily, had she been there; that poor little girl missed her father so much more than answers and words could ever possibly set right.

But later, he had realised.

Perhaps the time for words had passed – Morris had always been better at action anyway: doing, being, living...

So he had made his list, started gathering his tools, fired up the computer – even ignored the phone. He would call Jonathon back later; would spend all night mastering e-bay if he had to.

Because right now, old fool or not, Morris had hearts to mend.

And once again, Lily and her book had shown him the way.

*

Darling Michael –

It's a miracle. I didn't think those could happen anymore, not without you – because how could miracles exist in the same world that took you away? But this morning... well, there's no other way to describe it.

I'd barely slept, again – although not from Lolly's screams and cries in the night anymore. She hasn't had nightmares since Mr Woods gave her his wife's book, since she learnt about Wonderland. He's helped us so much, Michael, in his quiet, unassuming way – Lolly talks endlessly now, about him and his wife, about all Alice's adventures... Even about you. I was scared she would never speak again; she's still not quite the same. Few smiles light her up like they used to. But then, I guess no smiles light me up either.

And I can't forget her question, the one she asked Mr Woods last week – whether people could go to Wonderland, whether there were "Lollies" there. He knew what she meant, Michael, as much as I did. And I knew she missed you, how could she not? You're her hero, her Daddy... But she wants you back, enough to follow you to Wonderland, although she has no idea what that really means. I think, for Laura, it's all a story that will end happily when she wakes up.

I woke up the day you died – I guess that's why I don't sleep anymore.

God, Michael, I've worried so much about how to explain to her that she can't go to Wonderland too, that you're not part of a story... That our lives are here now, while you're...

But then – this morning, in the kitchen, stirring Lolly's porridge, I pulled up the blinds and glanced out absently. And it was like you were there, I don't know how... But it's exactly the sort of thing you would do, just for Laura, exploding her dreams into glorious technicolour – telling her, telling us both, that it will all be okay.

The garden was Wonderland, Michael. I know how crazy that sounds, but it was. There were patchwork rugs in the middle of the lawn, covered with numberless roses and jam tarts, glistening jelly in the morning light. Different hats – top hats, sun hats, caps, trilbies – studded the bushes, the bench, the trees. There were croquet hoops and balls and mallets, and sticking up out of the ground everywhere were bunches of those huge, sugar-striped lollipops and candy-canes you can get by the beach, gathered up with colourful ribbons and clumped together everywhere, a tea-party of sweets.

And the oak, where you hung her swing – every branch, every twig, Michael, was strung with more of those lollies; there was ribbon festooned everywhere, and gaudy sugared baubles of red and

43

green and blue and pink, until the tree was a multicoloured mass of candy-striped rainbow treats, all shimmering and refracting in the dewy sunshine. It was beautiful – completely mad and...

And completely you.

Her face lit up, Michael, when she saw all those lollipops from Wonderland.

Our little Lolly smiled and smiled; she took my hand and we raced outside... Her Daddy was written in every single tiny detail, back with us, and she just beamed at me, in my arms – no tears, just... wonder.

In that moment, I knew; we're going to be okay. Topsy-turvy, back-to-front, upside-down, shattered in pieces and glued back together... Somehow, we're going to be okay.

Because really it's all Wonderland, isn't it, Michael?

*

Morris Woods genuinely didn't hear the phone ring that morning, nor did he see the excited tea party taking place in the Winsor's adjoining yard, as the young widow and her young daughter danced and laughed through the colourful picture-book scene of their garden.

Instead, he was snoring quietly, contentedly, in a deckchair on the back porch. The rising beams of the sun glinted off a mass of translucent wrappers, skittering around the chair legs, while a tell-tale trail of baby-blue silk ribbon dangled languidly from one hand.

Around him, flowers began to unfurl against the green backdrop of Lily's rose-bushes; their crimson petals stretching like smiles amidst the gales of rusty, happy laughter drifting over the fence from next-door.

The Stone Fox

Robert Penrose was out of ideas.

That thought came to him as the taxi rumbled up the flagstone path to the daunting manor house front.

Set back in the Cheshire countryside the Hartstone estate was a modest Tudor manor house, made up of tiered floors with blacked out liquorice windows and peacocks colouring its gardens. Robert had seen its black and white patterned front before, but only in the brochure. It had been ranked highly in Writer's Annual's top 100 inspirational places, and was regarded as one of the most impressive privately owned estates in Cheshire.

Robert had taken all of this into account when he had booked his place at the writer's retreat. Held twice a year, and mainly filled with elderly novelists with similarly old and tired ideas, the retreat's aim was to gather writers with a struggling muse to share ideas and bask in the historic atmosphere of the house.

Robert thought it was a terrible idea.

His agent had been insistent, threatening him with all manner of consequences if he hadn't ventured further in his ideas for future titles. Of course, Robert wasn't convinced the ideas were going to come. Half formed genius plagued his mind and then disappeared; leaving the once bestselling author lost and useless, like a pen without ink. He didn't hate the idea of the retreat, but he had no confidence in it, or in himself.

The cab pulled up at the house front, where a red faced woman in her sixties came bustling out to greet him. Her grey hair was knotted into a haphazard bun, with strays sticking out at mad angles, quite a contrast to the spotless summer dress she wore; yellow with floral pattern, overlaid by a frilly white apron.

Robert emerged from the car, giving her a rather nervous look. At forty, Robert was going to stick out like a sore thumb as the youngest - and that was saying a lot.

'Welcome to Hartstone House,' the slightly erratic woman proclaimed, presenting herself to Robert with bright, friendly eyes and a welcoming smile. 'Are you here for the retreat?'

'I'm here for ideas,' Robert smiled, shifting his backpack higher up his shoulder.

'We should have plenty of those here,' the woman replied, gesturing back to the house. 'I'm Agatha Reed. I run the house while the owners are away. Make yourself at home, we'll register you and get you to your room, shall we?'

They went inside, chatting quietly; Robert introduced himself, and explained to Agatha that he really wouldn't normally attend something like this, and made bitter jokes about how he was out of ideas anyway, and it was all rather pointless. Agatha laughed, presenting him with the register, which Robert signed in a scrawl.

The interior of the house was rustic, with no attempt at modernisation. Robert had always liked that about stately homes: the obsession with keeping things ancient, time locked in their era. It was a love letter to the past, and Hartstone House was no different.

Wooden beams stretched across the ceiling like strings in a piano, spidery arms holding it at bay, and wall sconces cast orbs of orange over patterned walls.

There were doors leading off from left to right, beckoning guests to new wonders of old, charming Robert with their low hanging frames and aging, pocked wood. The entrance hall itself was laid out like a day room of sorts, with sofas and sunken pillows, long necked lamps watching over all; it gave off a warm, welcoming atmosphere, opening its elderly arms to visitors.

Robert decided that this wouldn't be a bad place to spend his weekend, despite his wishes to be anywhere else.

*

After Robert had dropped his backpack off in his room – high ceilinged, with a four poster bed and views of the grounds, stretching left to right – he headed back downstairs, armed with notebook and pen.

The ideas would come to him, whether they liked it or not.

Robert crossed over the balcony bordering the entrance hall, noting the fine oak banisters and the panelled, Rubick's cube walls. He was particularly interested to find there was a locked door along the way, perhaps added after the original build of the house. He made a note to quiz Agatha on it later.

Like any stately home, paintings lined the walls, ancient faces watching from ornate frames. Robert didn't follow art particularly well – he failed to understand symbolism or note the impressive brush strokes - and yet he could appreciate a beautiful piece of work when presented to him. Hartstone House displayed walls and walls of original artwork that widened Robert's eyes and slowed his step.

As of yet, he hadn't spotted any of the other patrons of the writing retreat, and that struck Robert as odd. For a few frightening moments, back in his room, he had wondered if he had been the only shmuck to sign up.

It was by coincidence that the first person he spotted was a woman, admiring one of the paintings with a degree of fascination that Robert would never have been able to employ. Straight blonde hair reached below her shoulders and round glasses balanced on the tip of her nose, illuminating blue eyes alive with intellect. She was focused on a notebook, scribbling away with a concentrated frown. Robert sidled up to her, too glad to see another human being that wasn't the erratic Agatha, and cleared his throat.

'Are you a slave to your imagination too?'

The woman blinked, evidently surfacing from a deep train of thought, and glanced at Robert.

'Actually,' she replied slowly, nodding her head towards the painting. 'I need to be here.'

Robert turned his attention to the painting – no different to the pieces that adorned every other hall, and tilted his head. The portrait of a woman stared back at him, with the tell-tale simple and pretty features of a Tudor lady. Wisps of brown hair escaped her headdress, pinning up the rest of her locks but failing to capture those at the front. Her hands were crossed on her lap, delicate fingers pointing to what looked to be a fox, carved from stone, tucked beneath the opposing arm. Despite the age of the painting, it's stark emerald eyes shone, giving what would normally have been a common portrait an unusual edge. Robert noticed that the woman in the painting differed to others he had seen in similar paintings – she was modest, and yet slightly rough around the edges, not a prim, perfect representation like so many portraits from the era. He found himself liking her. It was the first time Robert had actually connected with a painting.

'Studying paintings, then?' He asked idly, his gaze almost constantly sliding back to the bright eyes of the stone fox. The woman beside him tucked her pen behind her ear.

'Not especially. I'm actually here to write a book on the house, and its family history,' she nodded towards the portrait. 'It all begins with the stone fox.'

Robert raised his eyebrows, interest piqued; he held a hand out to his new acquaintance.

'You'll have to tell me about it - and yes, I am using you as a form of procrastination. Robert Penrose.'

The woman smiled in good humour and took his hand in return, giving it a brief, but warm shake.

'Abigail Hayes.'

Robert inclined his head.

'Nice to meet another writer. Though I can't say it makes me feel any better, knowing you already have something to write about.'

'Hartstone House is fascinating,' Abigail replied, gesturing back to the painting. 'Particularly because of this, and the stone fox. It's the missing family emblem, has been since the persecution of priests under Henry the Eighth.'

'Worth a lot then,' Robert commented, leaning in and squinting at the portrait. Abigail nodded, but gestured away dismissively.

'Very, but worth a lot more in sentimental value, rather than intrinsic.'

Robert understood that, but he also understood that two emeralds would pay his rent for a long while, and in the world of writing, where nobody is quite sure when the next pay cheque is due, that was a godsend. He opened his mouth to inappropriately say so, when there was the sound of an old fashioned bell downstairs. Robert twisted to peer over the banister of the balcony; Agatha was below, waving a brass bell that belonged in a school playground, not a writer's retreat.

'The first workshop is about to start in the drawing room,' she announced with a red faced smile. 'If everybody would come along, there'll be tea and cake!'

Robert decided it was rude to deny that, and Abigail agreed. Together, they headed to the drawing room, side by side, a friendly bond formed.

*

'Procrastination is your enemy,' said the overenthusiastic workshop leader: a man in his sixties wearing a cravat and a v-neck sweatshirt. He gestured with his hands an awful lot, and each patronising nugget of advice he came out with pushed Robert into heaving a groan of disapproval. Abigail's eyes flickered to him once or twice, evidently a little concerned that there was something seriously the matter. Robert didn't understand why she had come along; if she wasn't a washed up hack without ideas, why had she followed?

He supposed she was laughing at him. Which he didn't blame her for; he was laughing at himself, too.

'Robert, how do you deal with procrastination?' The leader asked, leaning forwards and resting his head in hand, offering a quizzical look that Robert refused to believe was genuine.

'I come to writing workshops.' He replied dryly, and he was sure he heard Abigail stifle a squeak of laughter beside him.

To continue with his nonchalance, Robert took a mouthful of his scone, and the workshop leader hastily moved on.

'We'll take a short break, come back in ten minutes everyone, when we'll be discussing writing prompts!'

Another groan escaped Robert's throat and he got to his feet, joined by Abigail. She nudged his arm with her elbow, and nodded towards the kitchens. Robert understood immediately and nodded, leading the way out of the workshop and towards tea.

*

Ten minutes later, the newly acquainted Robert and Abigail were not back in their seats, but in the entrance hall, talking over steaming mugs of freshly brewed tea. Robert noticed the wedding ring glinting on Abigail's hand, and she noticed his. They talked about their home lives, briefly: Abigail detailing how she and her husband were trying for a baby while the book was under way and he worked to keep them ticking over. Robert thought that admirable, and felt rather silly when he explained that he and his own wife, Hayley, had decided kids weren't the way to go for them. Robert was closed in, almost selfishly obsessed with his writing, while Hayley was a high-flyer – barely home, always away on business.

There was a contrast between their lifestyles, but if anything, Robert felt he liked Abigail more for it.

It appeared the feeling was mutual as they both turned their attentions up to the opposing balcony floor, and further, to the distant portrait of the woman and her stone fox.

Abigail flashed Robert a grin, evidently noticing his wide eyes and the slight, curious tilt of his head.

'Got an idea for a story?'

Robert snorted.

'No. I'm out of ideas. I just like the painting.' He sipped his tea thoughtfully. 'You said it went missing – the stone fox. Reckon it could have been stolen?'

'It's possible.' Abigail drank down the rest of her tea, and set it down on a four hundred and odd year old table. 'The early Hartstones were devout Catholics so there wouldn't have been any foul play within the family, or their servants. If somebody stole it, they must have been an outsider.' She shrugged, almost sadly, her eyes dancing back and forth, as if in memory. 'I'd give anything to see it. The fox. But it could be anywhere in the world.'

Robert finished his tea, gesturing for Abigail to follow him up the stairs. His mug joined hers, and together they headed back up to the portrait.

'You said the fox was worth sentimental value,' he muttered, grasping upon earlier conversation, clinging to it, both as a form of procrastination and because there was something deliciously mysterious about the house, about its history. 'Who's the lady in the picture?'

'Catherine Hartstone,' Abigail replied in a heartbeat, and Robert felt impressed that she knew so much, that she could pluck it from her subconscious within seconds. 'Wife to Richard, mother to Anne and Phillip,' she idly touched the pencil behind her ear, obviously moved by the story. 'Such a waste.'

A chill ran down Robert's spine involuntarily, and he tried to cover it by scratching the back of his head. His eyes flickered from Abigail, to Catherine, to the fox, and then, to the one hand, that was curled up, with the index finger pointing above and to the right. Robert's eyes drifted, a frown creasing his brow as he looked down the hall.

'What's she pointing to?'

'Oh,' Abigail tilted her head in bemusement. 'I don't think it's anything. Often, in paintings like these, there's a lot of symbolism. Hand gestures can mean-'

Suddenly, and with a startling clarity, Robert was reminded of the door. He looked down the hall towards its shape.

'What if she's pointing over there?' He didn't wait for Abigail's response – she was blustering in confusion anyway. Instead, he crossed to the banister and grabbed it, leaning over to see the passing Agatha, muttering in exasperation as she removed the invading tea cups from the four hundred year old oak table.

'Mrs Reed!' He called, figuring that a little more polite, considering where he was shouting from. Agatha span around in confusion and looked up at Robert, before giving him a confused wave. 'The door by the painting of Catherine,' he continued, still making a ridiculous racket. Behind him, Abigail was hissing at him to 'be quiet', but Robert ignored her. 'Where does it go to?'

Agatha hesitated for a moment, evidently gathering her bearings, and then her answer to the question.

'It's the old priest hole, love!' She returned, her voice slightly strained from the shouting. 'We open it for the public on summer weekends!'

Robert was no longer listening. He span around, regarding Abigail with a wonder and excitement that almost instantly rubbed off on her. In a fit of giddiness, she took the notebook from under her arm, the pen from behind her ear, and began to hastily scribble.

'Of course, of course. The painting has been hanging here since the family were murdered, it fits in too well...'

'Murdered?' Robert, mid step between Abigail and the priest hole entrance, halted in surprise. Abigail looked up, pushing her glasses up her nose with her index finger. Her eyes searched his face.

'Found dead,' she replied, voice suddenly hoarse. 'Killed mid mass, during the persecution of priests.'

Robert's face fell dolefully. It had been thoughtless to become so excited about a form of treasure, considering the circumstances it had disappeared in. There was something awful, outrageously gruesome about the house now, and the over-imaginative, authorial mind Robert possessed insisted that tonight would be a sleepless one.

Abigail seemed to notice his sudden pale-faced change in demeanour but thankfully didn't drag him up on it. She brushed by, notebook under arm once more and pen behind ear, before halting in front of the door. She drew a bunch of keys from her pocket, which jangled and danced, and with ease, she selected one, and shoved it in the lock.

'I've never needed to use this,' she murmured as Robert joined her, 'never thought I'd need to.'

'So how special do you have to be to get a big bunch of keys to every door around here?' Robert teased, though he was genuinely vexed. Perhaps, because of the subject of Abigail's book, the Hartstones had allowed her complete access to the house.

'Pretty special,' Abigail smirked in response, and the door eased open.

Like an episode of Scooby Doo, both parties poked their heads inside. It was clear why the extra door had been added, now. With priest holes being created inside the cavernous walls of Tudor architecture, an easier way for tourists to get a view was with the modern addition. Robert was fascinated. He peered up the slim passage ahead, blocked at the far end by a small wooden ladder – all original wood from the era – leading up to the tiniest hatch he had ever seen. It'd be a tight fit for a grown Tudor man. There was the smell of age old dust, and the gloom of history, but it was exciting, especially now that there was incentive to be here.

The intrepid Abigail was already through the door and testing the rungs of the ladder before

57

Robert could comment. As she began to climb, she spoke softly, keeping her back to him.

'You become close friends with your priest, after a while,' she said, moving further into the shadows, using her smart phone to cast an artificial glow ahead. Robert grit his teeth, feeling nervous, but also reasoning that if the house were allowing tourists up there, it must be safe. 'All those illegal masses, always on the edge of your seat. The only thing you all want is to be close to God, but if you're found, you'll end up closer to God than you'd hoped.'

'Oh?' Robert squinted into the gloom. Abigail was nearing the top, and suddenly, now that she was compared to it, the hatch seemed smaller. He wasn't sure what they expected to find. The stone fox? A clue?

'I read that the Hartstone's priest became a dear friend. He was, ironically, the only one who escaped the raid that night.' She swallowed, and Robert could hear her shallow breathing. 'He painted Catherine in wake of it. From memory. That's his portrait.'

'Then it really is a clue,' Robert realised as Abigail crammed herself into the hatch, and began to feel around. 'Maybe he hid the fox up there.'

'Well,' came the reply, 'there's no way anything could be hidden here. It's a verified cave: there're no cracks or slats for any hidden compartments.'

Robert pressed his lips together. It was bad enough that he was procrastinating while in the Last Chance Saloon of writing holidays, obsessed with the idea of an emblem that had been long gone for centuries, but now his only slice of adventure was diminishing. He couldn't have that. Like chasing the lines of a story to the finish, Robert had to finish this, too.

'You're right, no space,' he replied, pulling out his own phone. 'Unless he wanted to leave a clue.' It was a long shot, but now Robert Penrose was Indiana Jones, and he had to scour the place for something, anything that could be a veritable reason to stay away from the hippy writing work shop back there.

He dropped to his knees, and began at the lowest rung of the ladder, the only part of the remaining priest hole that hadn't been restored or removed. The wood was cracked and ancient, perfect for sliding in messages.

Like a forensic scientist, Robert concentrated, using the glow of his phone screen to investigate each step he came across. Higher, higher, using his room key to slide in and out of any cracks he found, Robert ended up at the final step before the hatch itself, just as Abigail's tousled blonde head popped out.

'What're you doing?'

'I'm Lara Croft,' he replied, and then hastily checked himself. 'Indiana Jones. CSI division,' and on that word, the key in the final crack poked browning parchment from the confines of wood, and Robert's breath caught in his throat. 'Jesus…'

Abigail dangled from the hatch, peering down at the slip of parchment as Robert pulled it free with delicate fingers. Her breathing had doubled, and even in the gloom Robert could see that she was quivering with excitement.

'Oh my God…'

It was a ridiculous idea, to open a historical artefact in a priest hole that really, they shouldn't have been in, when any of the attending writers could pass by and poke their heads in. Robert felt oddly protective and selfish about the paper, and his and Abigail's adventure. He hadn't felt so alive in such a long time, not since his writing drip had run dry.

With fingers that only just stayed steady, Robert unfolded the paper and smoothed it onto the flat surface of the rung. In fine scrawl, dated 1534, was a small message that would change the lives of Abigail Hayes and Robert Penrose, and the history of Hartstone House, forever.

Dear Catherine and her beloved family remain on Hartstone ground.
Beyond the stone foot bridge and in coils of holly are my protectors.
Rest well.

Abigail's breathing had stopped altogether and Robert realised, on one particularly heavily intake, that his had also.

'Oh my God, he buried them. He buried them in the house grounds. But, but how have they not been discovered?' Abigail whispered, evidently only a couple of revelations away from fainting. Robert noticed her fiddling, pulling off her glasses, wiping them of dust, or twisting her wedding ring.

'I think a patch of holly is enough to ward anybody off, and if it's far enough in the grounds, it won't necessarily have been dragged up.' Robert replied thoughtfully, his own heart setting up a rapid beat of adventure and excitement. Already his mind felt alive with ideas and wonder, and he realised with delight that his muse was signalling its return.

Abigail had taken the paper in hand, and was reading it over and over again, her eyes glistening.

'The bodies were never found. There was blood, a lot of it, but no bodies, and now I know why…' Her voice became a disbelieving whisper. 'Now I know why.'

Robert began to descend the ladder, knowing that if they didn't act quickly, time would slip through their fingers, and they would no longer be on an intrepid adventure, but stuck on the plastic chairs of the workshop space.

'If we're going to do this, we're going to do this now,' he muttered, glancing up at Abigail with sharp eyes. 'Are you coming?'

She regarded him for a moment or so, with an expression that highlighted her difficulty to fathom the situation, let alone the request. Robert wondered why it meant so much to her, why the family history was precious, something she heralded and polished, and spent so much time on.

'Abigail,' he insisted, holding a hand out, and his voice held a burning need that must have snapped Abigail from her reverie. 'They're waiting for you.'

*

Abigail and Robert ventured out into the grounds of the house, which stretched almost as far as the eye could see; territorial borders of trees sprouting in the distance and rising up like mushrooms. It was the height of spring, and the beds of flowers had been tended to with care: daffodils and tulips were sitting in fine rows, faces turned to the sky, green leaves held high as if hailing the sun.

There was the ever cliché 'Pride and Prejudice' fountain within view of the dining room, and Abigail and Robert hastily circled it, the running water from the high, grey plinth providing an oddly calm soundtrack to the valiant context of the duo's mission.

Down through the greenery, so beautifully set against a cloak of blue sky with waves of cloud, Robert flicked through images on his phone, frowning down thoughtfully at the screen.

'North of the fountain, keep walking. We should come to the bridge,' he glanced up, and gestured haphazardly ahead of them, into the jungle of trees and conifers. 'I reckon Catherine liked to have a wander after dinner, down to the stream and the bridge. It'd make a lovely walk,' he took in his surroundings for a moment, feeling a rush of inspiration abruptly take hold, and he took a contented breath. 'Still is.'

Abigail was mostly silent as they walked, barely taking in the carefully preened gardens and the barrage of colours. Robert had hoped that they would rouse her somewhat, but she was lost in her world of history, in the world of the Hartstones and Robert almost felt it would be a crime to disrupt her from that.

It was a good ten minutes later when they finally came across the bridge, which was obviously as old as the house itself. Its cobbled form arched over the running stream, pretty and ancient, a game of dominoes stacked up and curved lovingly over the rush of water beneath. Robert could almost see it in one of his novels: a secret meeting point for persecuted lovers, or the one last memory of childhood for troubled adults.

'Look!' Cried Abigail, and this time it was Robert who was torn from the hedge maze of his mind. He followed her quivering finger to see a dainty path ahead, leading through a surrounding battlefield of holly bushes. It had been left this long for beauty, that much was obvious: viciously pointed leaves shone emerald with afternoon sunlight, stray leaves and twigs created a floor of cracking, rustling woodland and Robert stepped over them to get closer, to look back and forth between the armies of bushes.

'It'll take too long,' he murmured, looking back and forth. 'God, four people went missing, just four. The graves weren't found for hundreds of years, I wonder why?' He was suddenly sarcastic, tired, and concerned that this had all been for nothing.

'Well, I'm not giving up now,' Abigail muttered, and she took up the biggest branch she could find, and began circling the clumps of holly bushes, poking and parting and probing. Robert watched her dubiously for a moment, but he knew she was right. The passion they shared for their adventure wasn't to be ignored, and Robert hadn't felt this inspired in years. He'd be damned if he was going to let this slip by.

It should have felt stupid, searching around like they were, but the note from the priest had been so real, Robert refused to believe they were on a wild goose chase.

'So he must have loved them, to have gone to all this effort?' He called, pricking himself on a particularly nasty batch of holly and swearing under his breath. Abigail laughed in return, a tinkling giggle that sounded more alive than it had when he had met her this morning.

'Imagine what you go through for your religion? Protecting, feeding, housing your priest? They were a good family, the Hartstones. They would have made anybody feel at home, always. It wouldn't have been difficult for the priest to become close.'

'What was his name?' Robert asked, and he was suddenly highly aware that he had never really considered this man's name, despite the amazing things he had done for his faith, and for the family he had trusted with his life. Abigail gave a crestfallen shake of her head.

'His name isn't written anywhere, not in records, not in history books. They protected his identity to the end.' She faltered for a moment, and then gasped, loud enough for Robert to know why.

He turned and streaked back to her, his hands red raw and scratched, a fine sweat beading on his brow. Already he was a shadow of his crisp self from the moment he had arrived at Hartstone House – clean shaven, fresh-as-a-daisy Robert Penrose was now sweating, lank haired scruffy-and-smelly Robert Penrose. It wasn't a pretty picture, but the latter was far more interesting.

Abigail had managed to create a small hole beneath the holly, and as Robert dropped to his knees and peered in where she indicated, he found what they had been looking for.

To anybody else, it would have looked like nothing – makeshift headstones of stone jutting out of the ground at odd, tilting angles, teeth in a decaying mouth; they were only small, evidently made from rocks found around the area - makeshift graves, certainly, with a solitary 'H' roughly and crudely carved into each front, marking the body beneath.

In his mind's eye, Robert could see the unnamed priest – gathering what he needed and running himself ragged, cutting himself to ribbons on the leaves as he cleared the way to bury his family. Robert only respected him more for doing such a selfless act, and allowing himself to be lost in time. He imagined that all of those hundreds of years ago, the holly was not so great in number and thickness, and it had bordered the graves prettily, but it was too hard to tell. It was fascinating, and beautiful: the miniature plot had been blanketed over time, the house protecting its past.

Abigail was on her haunches, her bloodied hands held over her mouth. Robert could hear her shallow breathing, he could see the tears in her eyes, smeared over her dirty cheeks, and he ventured to put a companionable arm around her.

'After all this time,' she said softly, the touch rousing her speech. 'My family.'

For a second, it didn't quite register - what Abigail had said. For a stupid moment, Robert's mind faltered and stumbled over itself, telling him that Abigail's second name was Hayes - and then he remembered the glinting ring on her finger. Of course, Hartstone needn't just be her maiden name, it could be a name long forgotten now, in her family, but still there, in her blood. The book, the research, the bunch of keys... Oh, how it made sense to Robert now.

He was no Arthur Conan Doyle, but at that moment he wished he was, because he felt ridiculous. His only question was that of how the family had lived on if they had been killed before they could have a future, but he mentally told himself that he would ask that later, at a more appropriate time.

His arm tightened around Abigail, and he allowed her to cry silent, overwhelmed tears, and while she did, his eyes focused on the small doorway into the past, right in the holly, and then they focused some more, widening as something else came into view: another shape in the shadowy depths of the holly prison.

He shook Abigail a little, and she wiped her eyes hastily, taking in a deep breath and whispering 'what is it?' with that same curiosity he so admired.

'Well,' Robert said slowly, feeling proud and almost wickedly delighted that he had found something too. 'It may not have its emerald eyes anymore, but...' He gestured, and Abigail looked; together they shared a grin.

The stone fox sat behind the four graves, like a guardian angel, watching with its stout body and pointed ears, even after countless centuries. It smiled bravely, every bit as remarkable as it had been with jewelled eyes.

*

The papers got a hold of the story quickly, and the house rode the band wagon of success. Suddenly, there were more open days, sold out to reams of tourists with snapping cameras and ecstatic smiles. The remaining Hartstones – great aunt and uncle of Abigail – came home to the news, and were more than happy to open the house to the public for extra days in summer, delighted to see the house attract such attention and life.

The Hartstone family had expanded past Catherine and her husband; the siblings of the family taking over the house after the disappearances - and of course they had respected the wishes of the priest to have his portrait placed up in the gallery. There it had stayed until the weekend of the writer's workshop, and there it would stay forever after.

Abigail wrote her book in a breeze, renamed it, re-themed it around the discovery over the cobbled bridge of stone, and it sold in its thousands, particularly in the proud areas of Cheshire that boasted its new heritage and newsworthy status. Not that Abigail minded. Her family had reached the forefront of history books: the tale of the priest and his love for his adopted family capturing the hearts of the nation. She remained in touch with Robert. They wrote to one another, and Robert even attended the christening of Abigail's new born baby.

In retrospect, Robert Penrose had to admit that he had been wrong about being out of ideas – and, regretfully, he had to admit that the writing workshop at Hartstone House had saved his writing career… though perhaps not in the way that he had expected it to.

His own book lined shelves and windows upon release, standing proudly alongside Abigail's, one fact, one fiction. Both brought the story of Hartstone House to life, and complimented each other, smiling down at history, with its heart breaking turns and heart-warming climaxes.

The stone fox was placed in the entrance hall to Hartstone House, welcoming visitors from it's podium, watching with staring, jewel-less eyes.

Because, of course, it had never been about the emeralds.

The Penny and the Biscuit Tin

'Good morning, Mr King; this is Nadia Dawson from the bank, calling to speak to you about the results of our meeting last Wednesday...'

Jim catapulted in from the bathroom, toothbrush still in one hand, and all but dived for the phone. Snatching it up, he managed to cut off the crackling boom of the answer machine, suddenly very aware of how important this call was.

'Hello, Miss Dawson? Sorry, I couldn't quite get to the phone.' There was a momentary pause down the other end of the line, as Nadia adapted her tone from the mechanical drill of a machine message to something more appropriate to human contact. Although, Jim reflected as he remembered their meeting the previous week, human contact was seemingly a variable term for Miss Dawson at the best of times. Personally, he blamed all this new technology – bank staff were now so used to hiding in their offices while their customers deposited their cheques automatically, or checked their balances remotely, that their people skills were clearly becoming rusty...

'Oh, hello, Mr King,' Yep, her tone was definitely flatter now. 'I was just calling to inform you that we've come to a decision about your mortgage application, after our meeting last week.'

Yes, you've said all this already, Jim felt like pointing out. He turned towards the large double-window that lined the exterior lounge wall, gazing steadily at the misted scribble of horizon, way off across the fields, to try and focus his nerves. *Just tell me the damn decision...*

'Right, so...' He trailed off, awkwardly crossing his fingers over the handle of the toothbrush still gripped in one hand. They needed this so badly, please, please...

'I'm afraid that at this time, given you and your wife's circumstances, we are unable to offer you both the type of mortgage deal that you would require.'

Jim felt as though his stomach had turned to rock, huge chunks crumbling away with every word Nadia Dawson spoke to plummet viscerally into a yawning pit of hopelessness. Obviously more accustomed to crushing people's financial dreams than Jim was to having them crushed, Miss Dawson continued to speak into the silent wasteland of the phone-line, stating the bank's "reasons". Jim, still reeling, only heard snatches of the same old tired clichés.

'I'm afraid that, in the current financial climate and today's... difficult... property market, even our best possible rate would require you to possess a minimum deposit of £20 thousand. And whilst you yourself, Mr King, are in a stable job with a reasonable salary, I'm afraid that your wife's situation... Well, maternity leave often extends

71

indefinitely in our experience – rightly so, of course, parents should be with their children... But – I'm afraid that it does leave your combined income somewhat less secure for the foreseeable future. Given that, on top of this, your ability to buy a property would hinge completely on your being able to sell your own flat – I'm very sorry, Mr King.'

If Nadia Dawson were any more afraid, any more "sorry", she'd surely quail with melancholy right there in her plush leather office.

How could they do this?

Jim drew in another deep breath, his fist now clenched around the useless toothbrush so hard his knuckles turned white. He stared out of the window, over the five-storey drop below their small concrete balcony and the spread of toy-town houses and patchwork fields that stretched into the distance, hardly seeing any of it.

The sickening, churning, falling sensation didn't go away though.

'Of course, we realise that this outcome will not be the answer you and Mrs King were hoping for – so we'd be very happy to arrange another appointment with you, Mr King, to discuss your options on what to do next?'

Unable to stop the heavy sigh weighing on his chest, Jim thunked his head forwards against the glass of the window and closed his eyes, resigned.

'Yes, sure – I'll... talk it all over with my wife and we'll get back to you, okay?'

'That would be fine, Mr King.' Now that the conversation was reaching an end, Nadia Dawson definitely sounded cheerier. So she should, Jim thought darkly. She was dodging a bullet – very likely, she would arrange it so that another colleague would meet with them when they next went back to that pit of bureaucratic despair that called itself a bank, passing them from one faceless mortgage advisor to the next, until they finally gave up this hopeless dream of escaping their tiny flat and living in a house of their own. 'We'll look forward to hearing from you, then, Mr King. Goodbye now.'

'Thanks very much for your call.' Jim grudgingly replied, before the line went dead. He slammed the phone back into its cradle irritably. 'And of course, thanks for ruining my day, you incompetent bunch of...'

'They said no, then?'

Jim spun around at the sound of Erin's voice, caught unawares. He wondered how long she'd been standing there; judging from the tired expression on her delicate face, she'd obviously heard enough. With a sigh, she crossed to him, hugging her battered flannel dressing-gown closer around herself, covering her swelling stomach, which protruded out from beneath her pyjama shirt.

'Was it because of the baby?'

'Well, they said the maternity leave didn't help... But, to be honest, love, it just sounded like it was everything – she seemed pretty emphatic about the fact that we can't afford a house unless we have someone *guaranteed* to buy the flat.'

'But the estate agent said that we're probably going to be dependent on young, first-time buyers and they can't afford the price we're asking because – '

'Because the banks won't lend them the money, I know. Somewhere, the God of Irony is having a wonderful day.' Jim's joke fell flat on Erin's defeated expression. Sighing, he decided he might as well tell her the rest; it wasn't exactly as if things could get any worse. 'And we need twenty grand in savings, not fifteen.'

'*What*?' Erin threw up her hands, dark hair flying as she tilted her head back to gaze incredulously at the lounge ceiling. 'We still have to *live*, don't we? What do they think, money just falls from the sky? I wouldn't mind so much if they hadn't been the ones to collectively gamble away the savings of the entire nation!'

Jim tossed the toothbrush onto the sofa and wrapped his arms around his wife, drawing her into a hug that was partly more for his comfort than for hers. They had lived in their nice, but extraordinarily minute, flat for eight years now – and, yeah, when they were twenty-five and still gloriously spontaneous it had been perfect.

But now, with all their friends comfortably settled in comfortable homes with comfortable broods of 2.4 kids, they yearned for a place of their own – with a garden, a second-floor, a hallway, a porch. They had wanted it for a good couple of years, truth be told, but they had always convinced themselves that the dream would last and that they could wait – for more money, more stability... Then Erin finally becoming pregnant had made them realise that the time was now – that *now* is everything.

If only the bank felt the same way.

Drawing back slightly, Erin looked up at Jim firmly, trying to re-gather her calm.

'We could always try somewhere else?'

He smiled gently at her optimism, but they both knew that the suggestion was out of the question. They had both always banked with their local branch, for decades now; they did everything through them. To go somewhere else would require a huge shift of loyalty, it would be a massive upheaval... and probably all for the same end result.

Nope, for now – unless money really did miraculously drop out of the sky – they were stuck.

As if reading Jim's mind, Erin squared her palms against the white cotton of his shirt and forced a smile.

'Well, I guess we'd better just make the best of it, then. Keep praying for viewings; keep squirreling away... keep buying lottery tickets.'

Jim gazed down at his wife and felt a surge of admiration. Somehow, she always managed to make the best of it and keep smiling, reminding him in her hopefulness to do the same.

It was just... He wanted to give Erin and the baby everything that was perfect in this world – to go home after a hard day's work to a proper house, one that they could spread out and be a full-sized family in, with a garden where they could watch their son or daughter grow amongst the flowers and trees... Somewhere that was private, theirs and theirs alone, with no creaking, whirring lift shafts throughout the night and a main door you couldn't admit guests through properly because the buzzer mechanism was perpetually broken.

After so long together, always just making ends meet, he felt it was time for them to have some real good luck – that one little boost to kick-start the life they deserved. But his God of Irony seemed to have other plans; ones which mainly revolved around kicking them while they were down.

Jim kissed Erin's forehead and then her lips, one hand tenderly caressing the curving bump of her abdomen. God, he wished he could fix this.

...Three Weeks Later...

Erin leant back in the reclining bed-chair hybrid that seemed to be a staple of ultrasound units, her t-shirt raised up to her ribs, as the doctor applied the gel to her abdomen. This was her second ultrasound, at eighteen weeks, and she still couldn't quite get used to the odd sensation of the cold smears across her belly, nor quell the small bubbles of panic that burst within her chest as she waited for the image on the monitor to appear...

What if something was wrong this time?

Her discomfort must have been obvious somehow, because the doctor smiled reassuringly as she gently pressed the scanner against Erin's abdomen.

'Don't be nervous, Mrs King; everyone worries when it's their first pregnancy. But usually any problems show up when we do the scan first-time around... This time you're going to see your little girl or boy growing a bit bigger – and no doubt just as healthy.'

'It's just...' Erin paused, worried that she was going to sound ridiculous. 'It's just, I've been really sick over these last few weeks and... I seem to have quite a big... bump... for eighteen weeks? I mean, I know it's my first time and I'm no expert or anything, but I have been reading everything I can find on the internet and the websites all say that the bump really starts to protrude around twenty, twenty-two weeks, which I'm not – and yet my bump seems quite big...'

The doctor patiently smiled at her again.

'Okay, Mrs King, well, let's get the sonogram under way and have a little look.'

Suddenly, the unreal sound of muffled beating filled the room, as if someone was drumming far away and underwater. To Erin, it sounded fast and thick, but then she supposed that it was emanating from inside her, having to pulsate through several layers of muscle and skin to make itself heard through the scanner. Coinciding with the heartbeat, the image on the monitor clicked into life, a world of greys and blacks and whites that all whirled together to form the hazy outline of *her baby* on the screen – fuzzy at first and as unintelligible as the static between TV channels. But then he or she was there before her eyes, a strangely formed, beautiful little life, secreted away inside of her.

Erin smiled – she couldn't help it – her happiness at the thought was overwhelming.

And then she saw the doctor's frown.

'What is it? What's wrong?'

The doctor imperceptibly shook her head, leaning a little closer to the monitor and pressing the scanner slightly harder against Erin's abdomen. The sound of the heartbeat seemed to seep into every corner of the ultrasound room, swishing out its rhythmic thumping against a swirl of fluid-sounding whooshes. The scanner shifted slightly across Erin's belly and she lost the image of her baby on the screen, the little warped figure disappearing into the blurring blacks and greys once more.

Erin felt the panic rise another notch, clutching at her chest with tiny fisted hands of its own.

'Doctor? What is it?'

Lips twitching, the doctor shook her head again, leaning back on her stool.

'Well, I think I can tell you why your bump seems bigger than normal, Erin.'

Erin noted the sudden switch from 'Mrs King' and the panic beat harder. But then, to her surprise, the doctor beamed at her, gesturing abstractly to the monitor.

'You're having twins!'

Erin stared at her; everything in the room seemed to stop still in line with her shock – even the baby's heartbeat seemed muted as her ears rang. Surely she had misheard?

'I – I'm sorry?'

'You're having twins, Erin – there are two little babies in there. That'll be why you popped out so quickly.'

'But – but... There was only one heartbeat?'

'Heartbeats aren't always exactly distinguishable, Erin – the babies are in very close proximity; heartbeats will overlay. Look, see – here's baby one,' She hovered the scanner so that the imager Erin had seen before filled the monitor once more: the concave hollow of her womb and then, curled up towards the bottom of the screen, the faint-tracing outline of a baby, not completely formed, but with the head rounded and the curled up body squashed below. 'And now I'm just going to turn it ninety degrees...'

To Erin's complete disbelief, the outline disappeared once again, only to be replaced by the outline of another foetus, pressed up against the top of the screen – same large head, same coiled body. Another little shift of the scanner and then the two whorled together for a second and Erin saw it – two little baby silhouettes curved around each other like yin and yang.

Unable to take her eyes off the monitor, Erin pressed a hand to her chest, her head spinning. Twins? *Twins*?

'How... How did we miss this before? At the last – last scan there was only one.'

'Well,' the doctor smiled at her evident surprise, 'your last scan was at eight weeks; things are still a little unformed then; plus neither you nor your husband declared any family history of twins so... Sometimes this does happen, Erin – it's very exciting!'

Exciting was one word for it.

Twins? She and Jim had never even thought... This was... amazing.

'So... are they both okay? Is everything okay?'

'Absolutely, both heartbeats sound normal – as far as they can be distinguished anyway.' The doctor hovered the scanner over one baby again and the pumping rhythm whirled and thumped out across the room, filling its mother's ears. Then she slid the scanner a little across, bringing the second foetus back into focus; the heartbeat skipped a little – or at least, gave the impression of skipping; instead, Erin realised, the ultrasound was switching across, the second heartbeat bursting the rhythm back into life, filling the room with whirly thuds that were just as vibrant as its twin's.

'Oh my God,' was all Erin could manage for a second and the doctor laughed, patting her hand. 'No wonder I've been so sick.'

'Absolutely; having twins means you have double the hormones, which in turn – unfortunately – means double the sickness... But they do both look healthy, Erin – they're roughly the same size and the heartbeats sound good and strong. You don't have to worry at all though – first time mothers who are expecting twins are scheduled for extra testing and ultrasounds so that we can keep track of everything and avoid absolutely any risk of complications. So we'll be with you every step of the way, okay, Erin?'

Erin exhaled a shaky laugh, still staring at the screen in amazement.

'Does that include coming home with me to tell my husband?'

The doctor laughed with her, patting her hand a second time, reassuring.

'It's always a shock the first time round, especially when you have no history of twins. But I'm sure Daddy will be just as excited – it's a fantastic surprise for you both, congratulations!'

Erin smiled, nodding without listening as the doctor continued to talk to her about tests, weight gain and other issues that they would need to schedule appointments to discuss as her pregnancy progressed. Her eyes were glued to the monitor and the profiled shapes of her babies – her twins – etched out amongst the static image of her womb. She felt she could cry with happiness – after days and days of worry, concerned that the vomiting and the quick swelling meant something was seriously wrong... Now they were blessed with not one baby, but two. It was a miracle – the first in months.

But was it a miracle they could really cope with?

She knew Jim would be ecstatic with the same thrill of happiness she felt – but even so, was this too much for them? After the failure at the bank, the thin trickle of their savings, the prospects of remaining in the flat indefinitely – and now with two babies on the way? It was small enough with just her and Jim for company; and their cash-flow... Besides, how safe would a fifth-storey flat be with infant twins?

Panic threatened to overwhelm Erin again, sinking different teeth into the soft folds of her heart this time, but still just as sharp. But as her heartbeat thudded in her ears, it mingled with another sound – the rhythm of the babies' heartbeats still thumping along on the monitor. Re-focusing on their little unsuspecting forms, Erin's fears were slowly soothed by the steady thump that swished like a muffled drum throughout the room.

No, it *was* a miracle – and the happiness that their little twins would bring would be more than a match for any other difficulties she and Jim might have to face along the way.

It would be okay.

They were going to be a proper family, nothing else mattered apart from that; not money, not houses, not endless hospital visits...

Erin smiled at her twins, heart swimming in a flood of love and pride.

She and Jim were going to give them the best possible lives they could wish for –

She just knew it.

The doctor began tuning down the instruments, withdrawing the scanner; the heartbeats vanished and Erin felt a little pang of longing rear up defensively as the sound was suddenly severed from her being. Slowly she sat upright again and, as she did so, was suddenly flushed with embarrassment as her phone began to trill from within her bag, down on the floor beside the bed. The doctor glanced up, startled.

'Oh my God, I'm so sorry,' Erin mumbled, hooking the handles with two fingers and flipping it up onto her lap. 'I'm sorry, I thought I'd switched that off - I realise - the equipment - I'm so sorry.'

'It's okay, Erin, don't worry.'

'No, really - ' Erin trailed off, frowning at the unfamiliar number on the screen, her thumb hovering over the off button. Who on earth would be calling her from a private number? The doctor caught sight of her confused expression and paused; then, patting her shoulder conspiratorially, she nodded her head at the still shrilly ringing phone.

'Go on, answer it, as long as you're quick - we're all done here, and I won't tell anyone.' Shaking her head in apology again, Erin flicked the screen to accept the call.

'Hello?'

'Hello, Mrs King?'

'Yes?'

'My name is Sergeant Warner, I'm with the Greater Manchester Police - Mrs King, I'm very sorry to call you like this, but I'm afraid your husband has been in a car accident...'

...Three Weeks Later...

As Jim grudgingly manoeuvred his mug one-handed, cursing the awkward plaster cast locked around his other arm from palm to elbow, he tried to remind himself for what had to be the millionth time just how lucky he was that the accident hadn't been more serious... A fracture to his wrist and forearm, five stitches to a cut on his forehead, whiplash, two bruised ribs from the seatbelt and an almighty concussion – it was an impressive list of injuries, but he'd take them all over a broken spine or irreversible head trauma any day.

And all because a guy paying more attention to his phone than the road had run a red light and turned a corner across the dual carriageway at the wrong moment... Thankfully Jim had only just shifted the car into second gear; going barely fifteen miles an hour, he had been at a slow enough speed for the incident to remain a 'minor collision' only...

Minor collision or not, though, Erin still hadn't quite recovered from the shock of receiving that police call, rushing to find him at A&E, scared and alone... She had been terrified; Jim felt a rush of guilt as he thought about this yet again. God, he had felt enough fear when he'd seen that Mercedes barrelling towards him – he couldn't begin to think about what Erin must have gone through whilst he was being brought into the emergency room, imagining those scenarios only ever contemplated in your worst nightmares... with the additional weight of pregnancy hormones to boot.

But it had been nearly a month now and he was recovering perfectly well. It was just the rest of their situation that was suffering. And that made what he was about to suggest so much worse...

Resigned, Jim cleared his throat.

'You know, I think we're just going to have to bite the bullet on this one.'

He glanced across at his wife, trying to gauge her reaction without obviously scrutinising her as he leant back against the arm of the couch.

Erin was stretched out at the other end, her feet tucked under her and a plate of spaghetti bolognese half-balanced between her ever-growing bump and the solid mass of a sofa cushion. She twirled her fork distractedly amongst the twines of pasta, chewing her lip; then her dark eyes rose and she surveyed his plaster cast pointedly.

'I'm not sure, Jim. I mean... what with the accident... something might still come up...'

Her tone was half-hearted; she knew he was right. Placing his mug awkwardly down onto the carpet beside his empty plate, Jim reached stretched out his uninjured hand and gently slid her feet onto his lap, rubbing her soles as she relaxed into him.

'I know - the accident was a setback we could have done without - '

'A setback? Jim, you could've died!'

'The guy ran a red and turned the corner at the wrong moment - at least I was going slowly enough for it to be a minor collision.'

'Minor? The car had a god damn dent the size of a meteor! You fractured your wrist and had serious concussion! The stupid tosser almost buckled the entire door off!'

'Erin, love - I know, okay? I know - and I'm so sorry it scared you. I'm sorry it scared me too, but it's over and... I'm still here, yeah? *We're* still here - and we've got to think about what will happen next, because - basically - things are a bit fucked.' Erin swallowed hard, face closing up. Jim sighed, his skin itching beneath the bandages. 'I'm sorry, but I just don't think we've got another choice, love. I mean – we haven't had any viewers for a good while now and the moron's insurance company is barely going to shell out enough to cover the car repairs, let alone compensation...'

'That accident wasn't your fault, Jim - I can't believe he's just going to get away with almost killing you and not - '

'Love - I know. But there's nothing we can do. Plus in another two months, you'll almost be at thirty weeks. That's seven months pregnant, Erin! By the time the due date gets any closer, there's no way you're going to be able to manage moving house, even if we were in a position to.'

At that she smiled tightly, spearing another meatball.

'If it meant having our little house, complete with garden and a stunning nursery for the twins, I'd find a way to manage, Jim, believe me...'

'But that's the other thing, Erin – we're having twins. *We're* having *twins*! It's brilliant for us – I can't even begin to describe how excited I am – but the bank aren't going to see it the same way... They were down on us before about the instability of our incomes whilst your on maternity leave – can you image Nadia Dawson's face if I tell her we're now having twins? Financial nightmare!'

Grimly, they both realised the truth of his words. They had no money; not really. The bank wanted a clear-cut deposit of twenty thousand pounds before they could even consider buying a house, whether they sold their flat or not – at that moment, they had only saved fifteen. And with the surprise of twins, not to mention the beat-up mess of the car after the accident, it looked like a good chunk of those savings was about to be rerouted.

Erin sighed, pressing a hand to her bump consolingly.

'You're right. I know you're right - it's just... so unfair. He could have killed you...'

'I know - but hey, I'm still here.'

'I love you so much, Jim - I was so scared! And now he's just walking away scot free and it looks like we're staying here forever in tiny old Flat 25, with no money and...'

Her face crumpled and Jim wished he could wrap his arms around her - *both arms*, not this stupid sling - and brush the tears away. It made him so angry - all this crap, day in and day out, but what did they have to show for it? A battered car and a fractured arm? A miniscule flat and loyalty to a bank that readily took their money, but really couldn't care less? Where was their dream house, their mortgage, their nursery, ready and waiting for the twins to grow up in?

As if reading his mind, Erin sniffed and looked up.

'So... we're just going to have to make do again, huh?'

Desperately, Jim tried to force a smile, swallowing down the fury.

'We can do up the middle room, make it perfect for when the twins arrive. We can re-paint; get some nice pictures, lots of teddies... I'll even take out that awful plasterboard fake-ceiling – we've wanted to do that for years anyway, right?

87

We can put in some nicer lights – really turn it into a proper nursery. Come on, love...'

She answered with the tired, but still dazzling smile he loved. Putting her plate down beside his, Erin shifted herself round and curled up against her husband, resting her head on Jim's shoulder. He slid his uninjured hand across her rounded stomach, the forced cheer evaporating as he realised, with unutterable tiredness, that they were fast approaching Hell.

'Everything will work out, Erin, I know it. It has to.'

...Three Weeks Later...

Erin slowly traipsed down the street, winding her way wearily towards the garage. The phone call she had received from them three hours earlier, regarding their battered car, had not filled her with hope – more with a leaden weight that approximated somewhere in the region of three to four hundred pounds.

Literally.

The mechanic, however well-meaning, had blinded her with science and engineering jargon, like *suspension completely obliterated* and *brake pedals gone* and *front tyre tracking warped*... Not to mention the crumpled door, shattered wing-mirror, and Christ only knew what other damage that idiot in the Mercedes had caused. But the three to four hundred pound bottom-line - well, that had slapped Erin down the phone-line no problem. She was still pretty impressed – especially given her particularly hormone-heightened state – that she had managed to refrain from cursing like a drunken sailor on leave until *after* the mechanic had hung up.

Jim hadn't exhibited the same restraint when she called to pass on the news however. This, on top of everything else so far over the last few weeks? Erin didn't wonder at her husband's frustration, nor at the air turning blue while they'd discussed which already severely battered credit card they would need to whack this charge onto. She was beginning to feel pretty blue herself.

Three to four hundred pounds.

God damn slimy insurance bastards.

They were as bad as the bank - worse, in fact.

She couldn't remember, through the haze of shock, whether the mechanic had said that the price included service charges... And what about VAT? No, Erin reasoned, he must have included them. She remembered him saying the phrases quite distinctly – she just couldn't remember whether he had said the words "with" or "without" in front of them... It must have been with, Erin prayed feverishly. If they bled any more money, they'd be drained completely dry...

But at least we're blessed with two babies, Erin chided herself, pulling her jacket closer around herself and her bump – more for the comfort of feeling cocooned than from the need for actual warmth. *And at least the car wasn't a complete write-off... And Jim - well, you can't put a price on life. After all, it's only money...*

The clichés rolled on, as desperately consoling as the familiarity of the streets around her; the retirement home, the converted bedsit, the row upon row of red-brick Edwardian terraced houses. They flanked her progress down the road, towering above Erin like smart-fronted guardsmen, mocking her with their homely frontages and cosy little gardens. Eight years in that fifth-floor flat; Erin dreamt of even the smallest of four-by-four straggling, grassy patches leading to her front door...

She sighed and picked up her pace, more clichés mopping up her melancholy. *It's not about the building, Erin – home is where your heart is.*

Perhaps it was because of the clichés that she noticed it at all in the first place.

Or maybe it was simply because, trying to avoid the tantalising sight of all the homes surrounding her, she had her head now permanently bowed towards the pavement, eyes fixed on the concrete blurring under each step.

Either way – there it was, lying on the pavement: a dull, glinting penny, tails side up, slap-bang in the middle of her path.

Erin saw it, but actually continued on two steps before it fully registered. Pausing, she turned, eyeing the unsuspecting coin thoughtfully. *Find a penny, pick it up; all the day you'll have good luck...*

Well.

She and Jim could definitely use a little luck.

Stooping, Erin picked up the penny and rolled it between her thumb and forefinger, feeling its dull, rusting surface scraping between her fingertips. When she was a kid, she used to love collecting surprise pennies like this one, gathering them up in her piggy-bank like sudden windfalls, until she finally had a couple of pounds saved that her Mum would swap her for, so that she could go and buy an ice cream or a packet of space invaders. Pennies were gold to little children; she hoped her twins would one day feel the same.

But suddenly – standing there in the middle of the street, surrounded by houses of which any would be like a dream come true for her, on her way to collect a car that was going to tip them into tighter and tighter straits after an accident that wasn't even their god damn fault! – suddenly, Erin felt faintly silly to have such faith in a dirty penny lying in the street.

Nonetheless, she slipped it into her pocket and headed on towards the garage, smoothing her growing bump beneath the folds of her maternity jumper and jacket. *You can't put a price on life*, she reminded herself.

The bell above the garage office door tinkled as she entered, before another bleep sounded farther back, announcing her to the various mechanics clustered in the workshop. Erin hovered by the counter, waiting as the owner bustled in, smiling warmly at her.

'Hello, my dear – sorry that I have to be the bearer of bad news.'

Erin steeled herself, praying once again that she hadn't got it wrong, that the three to four hundred pounds included the service charge, the VAT... With a sympathetic look, the mechanic pushed the bill across the counter to her – and Erin felt the blood leech from her cheeks. So the amount quoted on the phone earlier had been *without* the extra service charges after all.

Shit.

Swallowing hard and attempting to keep her face neutral, although inside a small voice was screaming, Erin double-checked the figure printed at the bottom of the invoice, just to make sure she hadn't hallucinated.

Seven hundred and eighty-two pounds.

Quite a bit more than three to four...

Could the service and VAT charges really make that much of a difference?

Her rapid-fire mental maths quickly worked out that they could and they did.

The garage owner watched her anxiously; he had just noticed her pregnant belly and was quite obviously panicking that the cost of the repairs might cause her to faint – or worse, go into labour. He'd probably be even more horrified to know that she was actually taking a moment to imagine throttling the life out of the little dirt-rat who had so recklessly driven straight into her husband's car. And every single one of his slimy insurance representatives. Why not throw in his arrogant little attorney too?

Grimacing out a smile, Erin cleared her throat and tried to see through the red fog of fury clouding her brain. When she finally managed to speak, she was amazed at how calm she sounded – perhaps it was a delayed reaction and, given another minute, she'd instead start sobbing hysterically into the man's overalls?

'You take credit cards, right?'

The garage owner nodded; at least he had the decency to look guilty, although Erin couldn't blame him for this...

Can't put a price on life, Erin.

As he moved to the till to start inputting the details, Erin took the car key from where he'd lain it behind the desk and fished a hand absently into her pocket for the rest of her keys, distractedly aiming to thread it back onto the bunch while she waited - anything to keep her mind from contemplating the truth of the situation: they were so deep in the red now, it was definitely the fires of Hell.

As she pulled the key-ring out, her fingers brushed something else –

The lucky penny.

Erin stared down at it, hysteria finally welling up like tidal wave.

Well, a fat lot of good you did me.

She weighed it in her palm for a second, the other hand pressed once more against her the curving bump of her stomach; the movement was becoming quite a comfort-tic now, part of her still unable to believe that she was carrying two little lives deep inside of her own body. It was the one good thing that she clung to... The thought was still lodged dimly in her mind when the garage owner turned back to her, pushing a chip-and-pin machine in her direction, the inordinate figure blazing from its tiny backlit screen. The device came to rest beside a yellow charity tin, the label studded with happy, smiling faces looking up at Erin appealingly from within a distinctly hospital setting: *Children with Cancer UK.*

Pressing her hand more firmly against her bump, Erin's numb thoughts finally slammed into focus. As she fumbled her purse out of her other jacket pocket, she flipped the penny into the charity tin without a second thought, before reaching for her credit card.

Our future might be screwed, but least my kids will have a home, she thought with a sigh. *So you might as well go to someone who isn't so lucky... Besides, our problems number somewhere in the thousands by now...*

They were going to need a lot more luck than one single penny could bring.

...Three Weeks Later...

'Erin, get back in the lounge!'

Jim ducked, using the weight of the sledge-hammer to swing himself back out of the way, coming to rest with his feet still on the ladder and his shoulders angled backwards against the wall. Ceiling debris crashed onto the plastic sheeting that covered the floor, huge chunks of badly cracked plasterboard fragmenting as they tumbled from his efforts to destroy the warped decorating skills left behind by the previous owner.

'Perhaps we should have gotten a professional,' Erin murmured, doubtfully, ignoring him. She was hovering just outside the doorway, munching her way through a sandwich-box of raw carrot sticks and cherry tomatoes. The twins were quite large now and Erin seemed to live in a various array of brightly coloured and extremely baggy knitted cardigans, craving raw vegetables every five minutes.

Jim swung the sledgehammer onto the step above his feet and sighed.

'Believe me, I'd have liked nothing better – but you know we can't afford it right now, love.' He risked another glance at the half-demolished ceiling. It might not have sounded like the best idea – smashing the plasterboard ceiling when they lived in a block of flats; knowing their luck, the tenants above them would come crashing through in a bath-tub.

But then again, what he was demolishing wasn't a real ceiling. For some inexplicable reason, the previous owner – a rather odd elderly man, according to the estate agent, who lived there for nigh on thirty years and had refused to move until he finally collapsed of a heart-attack – had decided to plasterboard in a new ceiling about a foot below the original. Jim could think of absolutely no reason why anyone would want to do this – it seemed like an unnecessary amount of fuss over something that achieved absolutely nothing in relation to the room. And it looked utterly abysmal – the plasterboard had been developing cracks when they'd first moved in; now it hardly took any effort at all to smash into it and bring it down. Jim couldn't believe they had left it for so long.

The old man was a little eccentric, according to the family; Jim remembered the estate agent's slightly patronising tone of voice, as he gazed on the fruits of his labour from the security of the ladder. *Not quite with it anymore... Apparently, he just kept saying he liked the room smaller...*

Poor guy was probably rolling in his grave now then, Jim reflected absently. Already over half of the false ceiling was littering the floor, sandy patches of long-forgotten dust floating down to shower everything with its scratchy, sneezey presence. Erin paused halfway through a carrot, her nose wrinkled at the chaos.

'Please, Erin - just go back in the lounge, okay? It isn't safe,' Jim shouldered the sledgehammer once more and descended the ladder, ready to shift to a fresh patch of plasterboard. 'At least the old ceiling will widen the room out again.'

Erin smiled at him, slightly forced but still full of ready agreement. What mattered most now were the twins and Jim was determined to do the best they could to prepare for them. That was why they had decided on the middle-room; it had never been used for much anyway – what with the dodgy ceiling and the way it only had one window. It was sandwiched in between their bedroom, which was at one end of the flat, and the open-plan kitchen and dining room on the other side; for the last few years, they had just stuck the desk and computer in there, along with a couple of shelving units, unable to think more imaginatively of what to do with such a small, cramped space.

But now it would work pretty well as the nursery – close to their room, and a reasonable size for two little children, to whom everything would seem giant for at least the first few years. And with the false-ceiling now almost fully ripped out, Jim was right: the room already seemed bigger, lighter, airier...

Christ only knew what the old guy had been thinking.

Anyway – now that he was finally getting it sorted, they could redecorate the room with what little savings they had left, then slowly put away what they could whilst the twins got settled – and maybe try and turn things around next year...

Well, needs must.

Hefting up the sledgehammer, Jim mounted the ladder once more and, checking Erin had disappeared back into the lounge, sucked in a breath before slamming the flat wedge of metal into a new portion of false-ceiling. Dust flew everywhere and the plasterboard shuddered, cracks spreading outward like snaking cobwebs, splitting apart and crumpling in on itself until finally collapsing to the floor with a creaking groan.

Only one crack split further than Jim had anticipated, shooting into the section directly above his head and widening with a *snap*! before he had a chance to react. Unable to do anything more than fling his free arm over his head and face, pushing his weight forward to try and retain his balance on the ladder, Jim hunched his shoulders protectively as a huge chunk of crumbling plasterboard crashed down on top him, splintering apart as it struck against him in a shower of powdered grit, bits fluttering to the ground.

Then something massive and metal smacked against the top of his head, hard enough to shoot sparks through the dust in front of his eyes. He heard whatever it was clang against the floor, then silence as the plasterboard storm quelled.

'Son of a – '

'Oh my God, Jim! Jim?' Erin's voice was wavery. 'Are you okay?'

For a second, Jim wasn't sure. Please God not a second concussion; his arm had only just recovered too, for the love of... Then he slowly raised his head, running a hand along the back of his skull, fingertips probing through his hair. He drew them back and didn't see anything concerning – no blood, no jagged bits of metal or glass or whatever the hell it was that had struck him; there was only dust, and lots of it.

Still a little dizzy, he descended the ladder to where Erin was waiting anxiously, ignoring his warnings about the room. Jim ran his hand over his hair again to try and dislodge more of the dirt. As soon as he reached the bottom, Erin threw her arms around him, the twins' bump pressing against him too, as if trying to join in the shaky embrace.

'Don't worry, I'm fine,' Jim reassured her, kissing the top of her head and drawing back. He leant the sledgehammer against the wall and looked around for the fallen object, adding with a small smile, 'Well, that's was an adventure, wasn't it?'

'What the hell was it that fell?'

'No idea... Here,' Jim located his mysterious assailant, half-perched and half-buried amidst the mound of plasterboard rubble. Crouching down, he freed it and turned it over, pausing in surprise as he held it up to Erin.

It was a biscuit tin – one of those old-fashioned ones, made out of metal with a hinged lid and garishly painted patterns engraved into the lid and sides. The name of the company, *Walkers*, was printed across the top and there was a huge picture set against a red tartan background, which had faded over time. The design took up most of the lid and depicted a man in a traditional Scottish kilt and sporran kissing a well-dressed, Victorian lady's hand. The slightly surreal words, *Pure Butter Shortbread Rounds – Net Wt 500g,* curved and looped beneath the border, with a little picture of a plate of biscuits in the bottom corner neatly summarising the whole thing. Jim reckoned it must have been from around the 1970s; he remembered his grandparents having a similar sort of thing when he was a child...

But it was bizarre.

'Why the hell would someone plaster a biscuit tin into a false-ceiling?' He mused aloud. Erin was still staring at it, the same level of confusion written across her face. 'It *must* have been the old guy who lived here before – you can't just accidentally plaster something as bulky as this in without noticing...'

Jim weighed it in his hand; it was alarmingly heavy.

'There's something inside.'

Erin arched an eyebrow.

'Hopefully not the original shortbread biscuits?'

Exhaling a laugh, Jim shifted the biscuit tin into the crook of one arm and prised his fingers under the rusted lip of the lid. After a couple of squeaking tries, it slowly lifted – and Jim nearly dropped the whole thing in shock.

Inside, carefully wadded together in small piles and balanced on their sides, were sheaves of old-fashioned bank notes. Holding his breath, Jim ran a finger across one of the bundles looped up with string, peeling them back in flip-book flickers to reveal the Queen's face staring regally up at them against a backdrop of faded purple. It was a small horde of ex-circulation, British sterling £20 notes.

'Oh my God,' Erin breathed, dark eyes wide. 'There... There must be hundreds in there...'

'Try thousands... *Tens* of thousands, Erin!' Jim was still reeling with disbelief. He tilted his head up to the demolished ceiling. 'Christ – I guess the old guy knew what he was doing after all.'

'But... Is it – I mean, do we have to report this, or...?'

Jim stared at her, a slow smile spreading across his face.

'Erin, we've lived in this flat for *eight years* – no one's coming back for this. No one even knew it was there! I think... I mean, of course we'll check, I'll ring the British Treasury if I have to but – I think it's *ours*, love."

Amazed, Erin started laughing, her hands pressed against her stomach, the babies sharing in the excitement as she threw her arms around her husband, the chaos of the room dispelled in their astonished, electrified happiness. Jim hugged her back, the precious, fateful gift of the biscuit tin cradled between them in sudden anticipation of their future together – and with the twins.

Tens of thousands.

Jim drew in a deep breath.

He knew he would remember this day forever – because finally, their luck was changing.

...Three Weeks Later...

'Good morning, Mr King; this is Nadia Dawson from the bank, calling to speak to you about the results of our meeting last Wednesday...'

Swallowing the last of his morning cup of tea, Jim stood before the wide double-window of their flat and gazed calmly out at the sunshine peppering through the clouds, a light breeze rustling the leaves of the trees far below. He could see the 'For Sale' sign outside the entrance shuddering slightly in the slipstream, but for the first time, Jim didn't feel a spasm of anxiety at the reminder.

'I'm very happy to tell you that, given your recent... good fortune... we have been able to fully approve the status of your loan...'

Of course you are, he thought with a sharp smile, glancing briefly at the machine as though Nadia Dawson might see his cynical expression and lose her syrupy tones. *The Bank of England confirmed that the money wasn't counterfeit and we're being given just under twenty grand - of course you've decided to fully approve the status of our loan...*

It had certainly been amusing the day Jim and Erin had gone into their local branch, biscuit tin clutched proprietarily, to find out what the procedure was in reporting a small goldmine of ex-circulation banknotes. Ironically unable to speak to Nadia Dawson, the young cashier they dealt with instead had almost goggled his eyes out of his head when they presented him with their precious *Walkers Pure Butter Shortbread* tin.

Apparently, their banknotes were almost as old as the tin; the figure imprinted on the back was William Shakespeare, which – according to the Bank of England representative the young cashier spoke to over the phone –had first been issued in 1970. And, apparently, genuine Bank of England banknotes that have been withdrawn from circulation retain their face value for *all time*, exchangeable at the Bank of England in London.

So, two days later, Jim had hopped a train, the precious tin stowed deep amongst a padded mass of haphazardly chosen t-shirts and socks inside a rucksack, which he had clung to like a dying limpet, until he finally walked in through the imposing doors of the grey-stone building on Threadneedle Street.

Unlike their local branch, the Bank of England tellers barely even batted an eyelid as Jim presented the treasure trove of crumpled notes.

Ten working days after that, their battered bank account had been credited with a windfall that they could never have imagined, not even in their wildest dreams.

Dreams that were finally coming true.

'We would like to extend to you and Mrs King our full variable mortgage rate,' Nadia Dawson warbled on and Jim turned to face the phone fully, hands deeply entrenched in his pockets to stop himself from snatching up the receiver and crowing triumphantly across Miss Dawson's honeyed tones. 'And we would like to hear from you as soon as possible, to arrange one more meeting in order to finalise all the details. I wish you luck in your house-hunting, Mr King, and we look forward to hearing from you...'

Jim's stifled smile broke into a grin as she finally clicked off; they didn't need luck in their house-hunting anymore, not since the biscuit tin had literally fallen into their laps, sprinkled in plasterboard dust rather than fairy dust, but somehow still just as effective.

Twenty thousand pounds...

Their deposit. The fifteen grand they'd spent the years scrimping and saving could go towards the twins, just like it ought to, but without sacrificing the dream home they so deserved as a family. Jim surveyed the flat that they could now afford to leave on the market for a while, shaking his head in an almost euphoric disbelief.

Twenty grand hidden in the ceiling all this time.

Crazy old fool had known what he was doing all along.

Erin appeared in the doorway, wrapped in a bright red maternity cardigan; she looked less tired these days, instead glowing with a happy spark that warmed Jim's heart every time he caught her eye. Crossing to join him, Erin's arms slid around her husband's waist, the twins muscling in beneath the growing curve of their bump as usual, and they smiled at one another, contentedly exultant.

They'd spent hours over the past couple of weeks debating why the old man had stowed the money behind a fake ceiling – stolen cash? An odd insurance policy? A squirreled-away pension? Maybe even a bitter attempt at screwing over his remaining family?

Who knew...?

All that Jim could really be sure of was that the guy had definitely known what he was doing when he whacked that plasterboard into place; that – and the fact that, whether insane or eccentric, he, Erin and the twins would be indebted to him forever.

As if reading his thoughts, Erin glanced towards the mantle-piece, where the *Walkers* tin was propped in all its metallic tartan splendour. It was empty now, of course, but they couldn't get rid of it – how on earth would they?

It was their future, finally sitting before their eyes - the game-changer, more blessed than a four-leaf clover. From the moment they'd discovered it, they'd discovered their luck too. Or perhaps, like the biscuit tin, they'd had it all along and just never realised.

Either way, that tin reflected their perfect day out of its shiny surface –
And the start of their perfect future.

Impossibly Lucky

It was safe to say that Alice was unlucky.

Regardless of what people said about 'superstition', about paranoia and obsessive cases of 'looking over the shoulder', Alice was, by the by, unlucky.

It wasn't as though she had done anything to merit that. Perhaps if you asked her, she would shrug modestly, and murmur something about the mirror she broke when she was twelve; although that wouldn't merit a lifetime of bad luck.

If ever Alice was running late, so was the bus.

If ever she was sent on a coffee run, the cups would leak.

The heavens were prone to open when she stepped out of the house. She was often ill on her birthday, and once decided to pull out of her lottery syndicate, only for the numbers to come up on that very week.

It was safe to say that Alice was unlucky.

On one particularly overcast Monday, she waited at the end of the queue in a local coffee shop, looking out of the window mournfully at the gathering black clouds. They crept in, like balls of dust blown about by an invisible vacuum cleaner, and Alice sighed.

The door to the shop opened, and cold air blew in. The next moment, a startlingly cold wetness splashed against the back of her legs. She turned sharply, holding onto the list of orders from the office - which had blown away more than once on her way down there - and regarded the man facing her. He stared back with apologetic eyes and impossibly messy hair that stood at all angles, more or less defying gravity. He shook out the rest of his umbrella, this time away from Alice's legs.

'Hey, sorry about that. The rain gets in everywhere.' His cheeks were flushed like fallen autumn apples, and there was something roguish and unpredictable about his smile that Alice couldn't place her finger on. She waved a dismissive hand.

'That's Britain for you.' She nodded to herself, and then turned back to the counter, ready to order her coffees.

Five minutes later she bustled out with them in hand; cups tipping and bouncing in their holders, but - surprisingly - not leaking or spilling.

Rain began to come down in heavy, fat drops as Alice stepped outside, and she hunched against it. Her umbrella lay forgotten in the cupboard under the stairs back home, and she sighed; of course. Icy wet fingers trailed down her bare neck and arms as she set off - until they abruptly stopped, a mere moment later.

'What right minded British person leaves the house without an umbrella?'

There he was again, impossible hair and eyes and… umbrella. Alice blinked up at her new shelter, and shifted awkwardly.

'You're assuming I'm in my right mind,' she pointed out with a soft laugh. Impossible looked amused, and nodded to the busy street ahead.

'Well, regardless, I think drenching you with my umbrella back there means I have to keep you dry now,' he shrugged, and the hand that clutched the umbrella brushed Alice's goose bumped arm. She agreed, and together they braved the rain.

The walk back wasn't all nervous laughter and awkward conversation about the state of the weather. In fact, as step after step was taken in tandem and less raindrops fell, the conversation only deepened.

Alice found herself setting the scene of her life: of late nights studying English Literature for the Open University, and early rises for her job at the P.R firm. Impossible said surprisingly little about himself; even when prompted, and like most first meetings, names didn't come into question. The only things Alice learnt were that Impossible worked in the coffee shop on and off, and helped people in his spare time. Therapy work, charity work, he wouldn't specify, but their lifestyles gelled and bounced off one another.

Alice's office block had a primarily glass front with sleek sliding doors at its mouth. It bore quite the contrast to the slightly haphazard woman and her strange companion beneath the umbrella, reflected in its polished surface.

'Well, thanks for the help,' Alice grinned up at Impossible, and she stepped out of the safety of the shelter, beneath the dissipating storm clouds. She hadn't noticed that it wasn't raining anymore, or that her coffee stayed put inside their cups.

'Pleasure,' Impossible smiled back and passed Alice the other four cups, snug in their holder. Their fingers brushed as she took them.

Alice nodded – not entirely sure what else to say – and she stepped up to the side of the road. To her left, a sports car revved towards her, and the rather unfortunately large pool of water by the curb. The wheels hit the puddle, kicking up a fountain that narrowly missed Alice. She hadn't made the effort to dodge it, but today marked a first. She balanced the coffee, swore at the retreating vehicle, and glanced back to see the already distant figure of Impossible and his umbrella.

Of course, she had forgotten to ask his name.

*

The day slid by, slowed down by the constant threat of more rain, and Alice found herself morosely photocopying sheets, drinking copious amounts of tea, and occasionally thinking about Impossible.

Sunlight streamed through the clouds when he crossed her mind, or perhaps, that was something she had imagined, to befit the happy train of thought.

The bus chose not to wait for her as she left the office. The driver was like most; dead inside. A bedraggled young woman hurrying up the street was nothing when the bus was ten seconds behind schedule; not that buses were ever on time, anyway.

As the metal cage of commuters pulled away, a black cab slowed to a halt in its wake, and out of it... stepped Impossible.

Alice let out a low chuckle of amusement; her stomach did that irritating teenage thing that was something akin to butterflies, and she smiled.

'I'd make a joke about you following me, but would that be too forward?'

'Nothing like that,' he replied with a nervous chuckle. 'It's just that all that coffee you were carrying earlier really made me crave a cup. Fancy it?' His eyes flashed, and again Alice got the sense that there was something mischievous and a bit brilliant behind them. She laughed and nodded, her cheeks flushing a delightful shade of magenta, and together they walked back down the street, up the way they came.

Along the way, Alice was reminded of Autumn walks with her first boyfriend, and then of hot chocolate in the kitchen after playing in leaves. The tint of auburn in Impossible's hair was set off by the autumnal colours of the occasional urban tree, and they both laughed when red and orange leaves fell and tangled in Alice's wild brown curls.

'Suits you,' Impossible joked as he twisted them free, dropping them to the pavement, where excitable pigeons gathered in hope of food.

In the coffee shop, they talked of hobbies. Alice told stories with great enthusiasm of when she had visited Wimbledon to see Murray against Federer, and equally, those tickets she had blagged for the Paralympic football. A lot of the central tube line had been down on the first visit, and Alice had very nearly missed the start of the game. It was typical, really, of her. Of unlucky pitfalls and knock backs, that never sullied her life, but made a mockery of it.

Impossible shook his head, almost knowingly, and sniggered at Alice's ridiculous shortcomings.

They sipped their coffee and Impossible told her about stars. How he watched them with his telescope and his local stargazing group. He thought the distant stars were more interesting; the ones nobody knew anything about yet. He grinned and said he gave them names himself.

Alice was fascinated by Impossible, but she could tell that Impossible was far more fascinated by her. Strange. She imagined he wouldn't be so if he knew about her guilty pleasure of eating Ben and Jerry's ice cream while watching The Great British Bake off, or her tendency to stay up until the wee hours on the internet; entirely avoiding doing things of note.

When the coffees had turned tepid and cold from Alice and Impossible's constant chatter, they stood up together and shook hands. It had been a pleasant day, and suddenly the clouds were bursting to reveal final flecks of sunlight.

The bus rolled up to its stop as Alice stepped up to it, and to her amazement, waited as she said her goodbyes to Impossible.

'Watch out for puddles, or falling leaves, or raindrops, or anything that might sully your day,' he said with a smirk, ruffling his hair idly with one hand.

'Keep an eye on those stars,' Alice laughed in return, meeting Impossible's grey eyes with her brown. He grinned at her, and leaned in to gently kiss her cheek. 'I will.'

His lips felt as though they lingered there, well after Alice had watched him disappear into city life, back into the dull charcoal of high rise offices and flats. Her cheek tingled on the bus ride all the way home.

Not once did Alice think to ask his name. It seemed that Impossible simply walked in and out of her life one day, and that was that. It was enough.

In retrospect, Alice could wonder why she hadn't done those things, but she never did. She barely remembered. After that day, though, the impossible seemed more believable. The coffee never spilled, the umbrella was never forgotten, and the bus was rarely missed. The days were brighter.

It was safe to say that Alice was lucky.

See No Evil Hear No Evil

They had been warned about the path when they first moved in; little more than a strip of stone-peppered dirt that branched off from a nearby forgotten field. The conifers at the rear of the garden, overgrown and thistle-twined, banked one side of the track for quite some way and a rickety fence lined the other. Only a few weather-worn walkers ever sought it out, and the locals, despite knowing vaguely of its existence, had no real reason to use it.

None, at least, that Anna Camm could think of. And, as a novelist, thinking of motives and stories was most definitely her forte.

It was a Tuesday afternoon in the first strains of March; spring had arrived early, without warning, like an eccentric great-aunt on the doorstep. The sun had begun to shine with greater clarity, illuminating each day with dappled beams that filtered through the mellowing fingers of the tree branches; a crisp wind tinted with warmth rustled through the hedgerows. The countryside was slowly greening over, bringing with it the promise of change and renewal, a preparation of sorts, for something larger and more intense.

Anna had known for some time that spring was journeying towards their neck of the woods, ready to throw off the blanket of frosty winter slushed over everything. She had always prided herself on being intuitive. It was in her nature; as she so often declared, it was only a question of listening and observing – she wouldn't be such a successful author if she didn't possess the skills required to conjure life accurately across the page.

It was this sense of spring singing in the air that had Anna out gardening on this particular Tuesday afternoon – well, gardening after a fashion. Managing to hobble outside on her crutches, plastered ankle now awkwardly stretched out beside the flowerbed, she was actually somewhat glad of the chore. Since she had slipped on black-ice three weeks ago, time had lengthened into endless days trapped indoors, slowly drowning in a sea of murder mysteries and day-time TV...

But now, sitting outside with a bin-bag of weeds trailing the ground in an earthy train a few feet away, Anna felt buoyed up by the fresh air and the bright view around her. Their house, their garden – all of it really was beautiful, in an old-fashioned sort of way. Perhaps she'd simply been watching much more daytime TV than she'd realised, but Anna thought their new home resembled something straight out of an Agatha Christie novel: 'The Hollow', perhaps, or 'The Mysterious Affair at Styles'.

Not that there would be any mysterious affairs here – she and Peter were far too busy finally, successfully, living their dreams. Churning the ground to uproot weeds in a dull monotony, the light wind humming a lullaby, Anna's mind buzzed in a synaptic frenzy of abstract thoughts: her storylines, her prospects, her life... everything – quite literally – under the sun.

When they had first moved to the small village of Harthill back in October, after discovering their dream house right in the middle of the quaintly rolling English countryside, the garden had been a tangled mess of summer's decadent excess. Leaves blanketed the overgrown grass, bushes shot out distorted limbs to snag anything that passed, whilst rose petals and laburnum chandeliers withered into soup. Ivy clung to the back of the house and the deck was a sea of littered fragments of nature.

But Anna could only ever see other worlds; ones that she and their future children – the twins with green eyes and her copper bright hair, and a boy with Peter's passion and Peter's smile – would play in for hours. The deck would be the pirate ship, the overhanging willow near the pond their mermaid's lagoon; fairies really would live at the bottom of the garden, and they would hear the Hound of the Baskervilles baying away in the countryside around them, as they solved murders aplenty...

Anna stretched carefully, twitching her plastered ankle, full of imaginings; her fingers itched to scribble them down, but she determined to finish clearing this bed of weeds before calling it a day. *Diagnosis Murder* would be starting soon too. Her partially written seventh chapter still stoically headed her mental to-do list as well.

Yes, everything about their house - and, of course, their beautiful garden - fired Anna's imagination, which was as strong as a raging inferno even when she wasn't trying. But when she'd had her little accident, it was almost as if, by breaking her leg, she had fractured something else too – her concentration? Her focus? Without the guidance of the outside world, her imagination had begun to run untamed; now it was almost too far out of reach to lasso back into submission...

She sighed, stabbing harder at a particularly stubborn weed.

Sudden footsteps a little way off jolted her out of her daydreams and Anna dropped the trowel with a start. Was Peter home already? Voices drifted across to her and she exhaled the unwarranted tension, smiling as she realised.

The path.

Of course; she'd forgotten all about it. That muddy trail that ran patchily behind the tall conifer bushes at the very end of their garden, the ones she was sat in front of now. The conifers were so thick and wild that, coupled with the sparseness of the rest of the countryside and the fact that their house was actually a few hundred yards away, those ramblers who did traverse the path were often led to believe that they were a lot more isolated than they actually were.

Anna retrieved her trowel, waiting disinterestedly for the footsteps to resume pace; they seemed to have paused for the moment, voices still discussing something earnestly. She had heard noises from the path only a couple of times before

117

now; once when the weather had still been quite dry in late October and she had been traversing the odd layout of their rolling expanse of garden with Peter, taking a break from unpacking – the crunch of boots on the dry leaves had made them jump, she recalled, keeping them on tenterhooks for strange animals or a shifty visitor, until Peter had remembered.

The other time had been during snow in early February – only a few weeks before her fall – when they had been drifted in; braving the icing sugar world outside, they climbed out of the kitchen window to make snowmen and wage war. Anna had been amazed that anyone could have made it to the path, buried beneath that crisp, inches-deep gleam.

The footsteps were striding forward once more, the voices now silent; probably contemplating their picturesque surroundings and the views that would await them ahead, Anna surmised, levering the trowel beneath another weed, before realising that she would need to dig down even deeper. The ramblers' progress abruptly cracked to another halt.

'Alright, this is the spot - let's get this done.' The voice was loud and close, suddenly so, and Anna jumped showering herself with dirt. Get a grip; rolling her eyes, she patted down her shirt and face.

'Why'd you want to meet here?' The first voice was matched by a second, which had waited, inexplicably, a few moments before replying. It was woman, dusky in a youthful way.

Anna, still concentrating mainly on the weed, vaguely wondered at the sense in that remark – their footsteps had been coming down the lane

118

together, they had been talking with one another only thirty seconds or so before, so why ask about meeting now? The weed gave and she bore it aloft triumphantly; the first voice, male, came again.

'Because I didn't want us to be seen together – or overheard...'

Anna looked up, frowning. What?

'But I hate this secrecy –' The woman began; the man interrupted her.

'Would you rather we were caught?'

Ah. Anna struggled to one knee, plaster cast awkwardly splayed before her, tossing the limp, straggling weed aside; it landed soundlessly with dead, flailing limbs beside the bin-bag that held its brethren. A burning flush fired Anna's cheeks as she fumbled for her crutches. Was she inadvertently listening to a secret lovers' rendezvous? Time to get a cup of tea and –

The next words were so enigmatic, so laced with deeper meaning, that they cut across all coherent thought, rooting her to the spot.

'So it's done?'

'Yes.'

'He's gone?'

'Yes!' The word snapped out loudly, like crackling frost over a fire. Anna, nonplussed now, felt a sinister prickle across the back of her neck. There came a rustling, shuffling movement; the woman spoke again, tone forcibly tight.

'So what next?'

'We cover our tracks.'

Anna reeled back, mind whirling. What was this? Because it sounded like... No. Was she, Anna Camm, listening to the secret discussion of a crime?

Forget *Diagnosis Murder*! What the hell should she do?

The woman was speaking again, voice lilting quickly; she sounded nervous.

'Are you sure it's finished? That he's really...'

'Of course I'm sure! He's not coming back.'

Oh God. Anna ran her hands desperately over the back of her neck, mind racing. They had killed someone; it was all there in their words – this man on the other side of her hedge was a murderer! What should she do?

No.

Wait a second...

The normality of a sudden, chirruping birdsong slammed Anna back to reality. How likely was it, really, that these were criminals who had murdered someone in or around Harthill, one of the most quintessentially English towns ever imagined? Unless she had been transported into a *Miss Marple* novel, this sort of thing just didn't happen. Besides, no one had actually mentioned death or killing specifically – they probably were just a couple carrying on an affair as she'd first thought, and her husband had probably simply discovered them -

'Oh, God, Johnny – we've really done it. He's actually dead...'

Then again, *Miss Marple* must have been based on something factual.

Anna drew in a sharp breath, leaning closer to the bushes, injury forgotten. There were footsteps, the whisper of fabrics brushing against one another, and then this Johnny speaking firmly.

'No one saw me, Lily. We've just got to be smart.'

'Smart? Miller's dead, Johnny! How did we ever think we could do this? I'm twenty-two, I can't be arrested…'

'No one's going to be arrested –'

'No one's going to go to jail.' Anna jerked backwards. There was a third person? Someone else was in on it – this murder of "Miller"! Anna filed the name away, along with Johnny and Lily's. What should she do?

'Right, yeah.' Johnny's voice was weary. Anna sensed friction between this new voice and him – maybe the new person had something on this Johnny? Maybe he and Lily weren't the brains behind this murder. If only she could see what was going on! Johnny's previous tone resumed, slightly stilted. 'No one's going to go to jail, Lily! No one knows, no one saw... And if they did, well – then we'll have to deal with them too.'

Anna clapped her hands to her mouth, muffling a fearful whimper at the malevolence in his tone. She staggered back, horror overpowering her aching leg, aiming to run to the house and call the police – but what would she say?

They'd think she was crazy...

Maybe she could ring Peter. But what if they left before he got here? Besides, he might not believe her – saying, amusedly, that it was just her imagination... Anna knew the tone – she'd heard it several times before, usually affectionate, but there were times when affection mutated into annoyance: for God's sake, Anna, you get so carried away...

No.

Not this time, they'd just said – !

A branch cracked beneath her left foot, loud as a gunshot in a still night, causing the tension that had previously been so palpable to splinter into sparking, explosive shards. Anna froze, her heart palpitating against her ribcage like a netted sparrow. There was silence on the other side of the hedgerow, razor sharp, as she hovered with baited breath.

Swift footsteps strode closer to the conifers; the newcomer's voice sounded spooked.

'What was that?' A plastically metallic crackle, like that of a moveable piece of machinery – or a weapon? – undercut the more disturbing noise of the conifer branches rustling and snapping as someone attempted to peer through. Afraid to even breathe lest this band of killers should hear her, Anna clung to the hedge desperately.

Another few seconds of sporadic movement, and then:

'Probably just a cat or something...'

Grunting murmurs of agreement swam through to ease her bones; her pulse felt heavy and painful, thudding in her ears.

'So what now?' Johnny's voice.

'We go over the next bit,' the newcomer replied; paper rustled. Anna could only too well imagine what he was referring to: the next stage of their homicidal plan – how to avoid being caught.

Anna closed her eyes, petrified. She was no longer the star of a charming Agatha Christie; instead she was descending rapidly and unwillingly into a Henning Mankell...

'Well, can we hurry up?' Lily sounded anxious, on-edge – tired. 'I don't want to have to do this again.'

'Just remember your positions, yeah?' The third voice distanced itself from the others, as though moving away; his tone definitely reverberated control.

'Look, Rick –' Johnny started; another important name for Anna to file away. Rick cut across him though, dismissively sharp.

'Come on, man – this has to be done by today; we really need to get the bloody thing shifted.'

Bloody? The colour drained from Anna's face. They were disposing of the body? Right there, behind her hedge? And less than an hour ago, she'd been imagining joyful pursuits of cops and robbers with her future children. Anna could feel hysteria mounting. Her thin frame trembled fearfully as she leant ever closer.

Lily let out a low despairing groan; Johnny's voice was tight.

'But Richard... All the bits –'

Anna's last fraught nerve snapped; bits? Oh God, they were butchers! And she had seen enough CSI reruns to know that it never ended well for those unfortunate enough to stumble across the crime. Fear flooded her heart; letting out a strangled cry, crutches flailing, Anna fled on broken bones back to the house...

Unable to shake the terror of ruthless, unseen eyes at her back.

On the other side of the conifers, the three Drama and Film students exchanged wary looks, the echo of the shriek carrying on the breeze eerily. Richard, camera-man and director, paused by the tripod uncertainly.

'... Probably just a cat, yeah?'

His fellow actors nodded hesitantly; maybe they should have used the college campus after all – it certainly was isolated round here. Anything could happen and you'd be miles from help... The dark backs of the conifer trees seemed to grow taller for a moment, overshadowing the trio.

Forget deadlines; that fading scream was too unnerving for words. What if this place were haunted.

Richard shivered.

'Okay – let's call that a wrap?'

The Hidden Dove on Hood Street

MAGIC SHOW TONIGHT
HOOD ST
10PM
£5 ENTRY

At first there appeared to be no words on the flyer, but when tipped in the sunlight, letters shone like lost contact lenses in a torch beam. Harvey spared a reluctant glance to his friend.

'People still do magic shows, then.'

Nick snatched the paper and studied it with a smirk as they walked.

'Never heard of Hood Street. Maybe we should go. Could be funny,' he folded the paper into a triangle, and obviously concealed it into his shirt sleeve. 'Abra Kadabra!'

Harvey quirked an eyebrow, but the spark in Nick's eyes were enough to make him reconsider. A few drinks, some tacky card tricks? It made a change from the Student Union. Could be an interesting night.

The mouth of the passage was reminiscent of a sewer pipe; the walls slicked with the slime of degraded waste, the path shrouded in darkness. Harvey peered down the alley, eyes flickering from exposed brick to leaking gutter. He considered the lure of the more central locations of his favourite bars, and grimaced.

'This isn't a street.'

Nick shook his head and gestured to a chipped and defaced sign. Through the filth and muck from years of pollution, the faint outline of letters could be seen: a message in the dirt.

'Hood Street'

'This is a great idea,' Harvey murmured, flicking a sceptical glance up at the surrounding buildings, which hemmed them in like the claustrophobic walls of a lift. Together they ventured forward, feet dragging in apprehensive scuffs.

There was only one venue down Hood Street, and even that was questionable. The only signifier that there was anything behind the boarded up windows and shuttered side doors was a low hanging sign, carved in the shape of the bird it paid homage to. It read:

'The Hidden Dove'

Nick had already knocked on the door beneath, before Harvey had chance to object. There was a beat. Harvey swapped an uneasy look with Nick.

A slat at eye level slid loose, and behind a metal grate, two dark eyes sized them up.

Harvey wasn't quite sure what to do. He shifted from foot to foot in an attempt to decide what to say, when Nick intervened. He brandished the flyer they had been handed earlier that day. The eyes narrowed, the small hatch snapped shut, and the surrounding door screeched open.

Red light leaked out from within and illuminated Harvey and Nick's faces in a mysterious spotlight. They stepped in, and a gloved hand appeared from behind the door, fingers wiggling. Harvey fumbled in his wallet and slapped a ten pound note down onto the palm. They descended the stairs, and the door closed silently behind them.

The Hidden Dove was remarkably warm and inviting on the inside. The ceiling domed; encircling and holding the occupants of the little club, almost as if they were in the womb. Small red glasses holding bobbing tea lights lit each table, throwing warped shadows on the wall and providing the only light, aside from that emanating from the stage.

Harvey looked around, all of a sudden feeling remarkably content and cosy as he regarded the tumbling folds of the stage's red curtains, and the tiny, rounded bar just to their right. The venue smelt musky, like the inside of a fancy dress box, and the tiny table lights were almost hypnotic. Nick rubbed his hands together.

'This is it, mate. Time for a pint.'

Harvey muttered something about cider and went to take a seat at one of the vacant tables. He listened to the murmur of voices at neighbouring tables: an old couple drank wine and laughed together, while a young woman twirled the pearls around her neck nervously with one finger as she chatted to her date.

Moments passed, and then the curtains on the stage twitched and parted suddenly, to a roomful of applause. Nick returned a moment or two later, and sank down into the seat beside Harvey. He slid a tall glass of cider over to him.

Somewhere, a clock chimed ten.

There was nothing on the stage, no props, no doors, nothing: until there was a 'poof' and a cloud of sparkling mist billowed out of nowhere, and in its place, as it dissipated, was the magician.

He stood arrogantly in front of the crowd, holding his arms out for applause. The people around did as his gestures commanded, Harvey and Nick less enthusiastically.

The magician was simply dressed: top hat, coat with tails. His white shirt was frilled at the chest and cuffs, unfortunately resembling the decorative trimming on a wedding cake. His dark eyes danced back and forth, the erratic flicker giving his otherwise ridiculous persona an untrustworthy edge. The crescent moon smile in his angular jaw was sure but false.

'Welcome to the show,' he drawled. 'I assure you all, by the end of this, you won't quite believe what you have seen...' Harvey sniggered; it was fun, very tacky, almost exciting. He folded his arms to feign nonchalance. 'I am Demas Boltof. And this,' he drew a wide scarlet sheet from within the confines of his jacket. '…Is my assistant, Iola.' He held the sheet up in a matador fashion, twitched and shook it on the spot; then he jerked it away from its place in the air.

Harvey sat up.

The casual introduction hadn't prepared him for this – hadn't prepared him for Iola.

Her hair was a cascade of warmth, flames of liquid gold that tore down her back in unruly, mad snarls. Her eyes reflected a mind that was whirring and thinking, always far away; her lips, full, red and heart shaped begged to be ravished with kisses. Her cheekbones were sculpted like the thin edge of a blade, drawing attention down to the hollow of her neck, and lower, to the soft curve of her hips, which pressed against the clinging fabric of her royal blue dress, like undulating sea currents.

Everything was accentuated, and yet everything was not enough.

The show went on, building from pantomime tricks – floating above the ground without strings, miraculous recoveries from severed limbs – to bigger, more impossible things.

Nick continued to drink and drink, sometimes cackling at the tricks Demas and Iola produced: rabbits that back-flipped into top hats, doves that emerged, flapping from the confines of sleeves. Harvey's pint remained untouched. The heavy beats of his heart, and the damp sweat on his palms and brow were more than enough to be getting on with.

Colours were cast above them, explosions and currents of neon, dancing across their heads like the Northern Lights. A pulse thrummed across the audience that rattled the ice cubes in drinks and upturned more than one hairstyle. A pair of boots walked alone across the stage, to which Nick murmured 'Bedknobs and Broomsticks' with amusement. All the while, Iola was either centre stage, lavishing in the attention, or in the shadows, watching the magic unfurl. Harvey's eyes revelled in her confidence, her poise and her playful banter with the crowd.

It was gone one am when the show finished, and Harvey waited by the stage, feeling stone cold sober and like something of a groupie. Nick clapped a hand on his shoulder, slurring something about Iola being 'a babe, really, really, you don't have a shot', before opting to stagger out of the club and back to the sobering comfort of his flat.

Alone, Harvey felt exposed and nervous, like he was about to step out onto a glass floor, with plunging heights below. It all worsened and bettered at once, when Iola came out – just as something skittish and firm brushed against Harvey's ankle. He had a moment to look at her: hair pulled up into a tight bun, with corkscrews of escaped madness standing out on certain angles. Her face was wiped clear, revealing more flaws, and that alone had an effect on Harvey, who followed her like a friendless child in the playground, hardly questioning what she was chasing.

'Tommy,' Iola hissed, dropping to her knees as the enormous back feet of a white rabbit disappeared behind a smoke machine. 'Tommy Cooper, get out from behind there…' Her voice was impatient, and Harvey decided that there would be no better opportunity to make conversation than that moment. He rounded the other side of the machine and caught Tommy Cooper in his arms as it leapt out. He grinned at Iola slightly, and her lips curved into a pout.

'That's my rabbit.' She said, holding her hands out and grasping pointedly at the air.

'I know,' Harvey replied, somewhat disappointed as he passed the kicking Tommy Cooper over. 'I got him for you.'

Iola's expression softened a little, and she rose to her feet.

'Did you enjoy the show? It's usually the older ones who wait afterwards.' Her eyes gave a dubious sweep of Harvey's checked shirt and styled hair.

'Yeah, amazing. Amazing… Looks like we've come a long way since Paul Daniels.' Harvey pulled out his house key, held it up for Iola to see, and then swished and manoeuvred his hands to distract her. The key vanished. 'Bit of Paul Daniels for you,' he said with a bold smile. Iola narrowed her eyes and then her lips curled at one corner into an amused smile. She reached out with her free hand and gave Harvey's wrist a tug. The key dropped from his sleeve to the floor with a soft clatter, and skittered away, out of sight. Harvey's cheeks went pink and he began to hastily search for it. Iola was still smiling, absently stroking her rabbit. She spoke in a curious voice, and Harvey ceased in his search to acknowledge her.

'What's your name?'

'Nick. No, wait. Harvey. I'm Harvey Morgan and I... came with Nick. We thought the show would be a laugh.' He was babbling and it required a serious amount of thought for him to stop. After all, her question had only been a minor ask. Iola wasn't complaining, though. She sniggered; a slightly unflattering snigger that suggested a less than dainty personality. Harvey found her all the more appealing for it.

'But,' he went on, all too aware of each word, each syllable and it's subsequent meaning. 'I think I'd rather learn about you. If that's not...Out of line.'

Iola studied him, and the sly smile became wider, warmer.

'Come on,' she said, holding out a hand. 'Demas won't mind.' Harvey remembered the head magician's sneering smile and untrustworthy eyes, but he forced his concern down. She might as well have offered him a pot of gold, or the Holy Grail. His reaction would have been much the same. Harvey's face ghosted over, while his mouth opened and closed mutely. His hand moved on it's own – thank God – and their palms slid together, fingers laced.

The rest of the night followed in a storm of wonder and colour.

Demas carried them away to underground clubs: places Harvey had never known existed, and almost, on retrospect, wished he hadn't discovered. There were clubs with women using poles like a lifeline; where shadowy patrons in forgotten corners welcomed new or known pleasures of all kinds and substances. The night whirled by in hues of desire and lust: purples and reds of the richest shades.

To Harvey, there was nothing worth his attention, not with Iola at his side. They talked mostly about him, which only made him ache more for her past, to learn about every inch of her. He divulged tales of his childhood. Times he had felt wronged and rejected, and went on about his parents constant arguments – and their subsequent divorce. He detailed his passion for music, for creating what wasn't there before, and highlighted his love for the unexpected.

They hid away in the quiet of a booth, while around them, sparks flew and drinks bubbled – more and more of Boltof's strange and wonderful crew gathering in the night. Tommy Cooper even bounced around their table, lapping up vodka and peanut crumbs.

All the while, Iola would only laugh and indulge Harvey with witty comments about his tales, never once specifying about her own life. Harvey gained confidence, and the eventual courage to tell her she was beautiful. She smiled like she knew.

'I love the performance,' she said finally, as the morning began to catch up with them and Harvey had finally managed to urge her words to surface. 'Learning to captivate a crowd, to hold them there. I feel as though I can do whatever I want. It's a well of confidence that I drink from every night. It's invigorating. That'll never get old. Not ever.'

At the time, Harvey didn't see the importance of that statement - of just how much it gave away. It only fuelled his fascination, and eventually ebbed and disappeared from the forefront of his mind as Iola led him through the door of her hotel room.

*

The following morning, Harvey pulled on his shirt from the night before, and as he buttoned it, he regarded the empty bed, the rumpled sheets... and the silence. The night before had seen a room with playing cards strewn across the floor, a line of devilish heeled shoes and eventually, the dress Iola had been wearing, along with Harvey's shirt. Now, none of that remained.

As Harvey descended the stairs, back into the hotel lobby, he reflected that one night with Iola wasn't what he had wanted. He realised that he would have been willing to give her one life. He questioned what he had done wrong, when the only thing that was memorable through the haze was how fascinating Iola was when she spoke... and how little that was.

Harvey tried, in a futile effort, to question the hotel receptionist on the location of the travelling show of magicians, but the female receptionist was insistent that there had never even been a booking in the name of Boltof.

Harvey left the hotel frustrated and confused. He opted to contact Nick on the subject.

>That assistant from the magic show. Did you catch her surname at any point?

It was bothersome that Iola hadn't even told him.

I don't know what you were doing last night, mate, but I caught an early one. <

Harvey frowned deeply. Had Nick been so drunk that he had forgotten where they had been? Feeling stung by the morning's reaction and all around confusion, Harvey caught the bus back home.

Aside from the initial trouble of being unable to locate his front door key and having to fish out the ancient back door one, Harvey got inside no problem, and immediately texted Nick back.

>The Hidden Dove on Hood Street-

He began.

>You spent most of your time laughing at the tricks like some kind of ape.

The reply took some time to return.

You're not funny. <

So Nick had had too much to drink. It wasn't the first time.

Harvey spent the rest of the day eating through bags of crisps, occasionally stopping to pluck the strings of one of his many instruments, or to shuffle the deck of cards he found at the back of the cutlery drawer.

It had struck ten o'clock –twenty-four hours since the show had begun – when Harvey found the number for the Hidden Dove online. Annoyingly, when dialled, the number wasn't recognised.

Harvey fell asleep by the laptop, pen in hand, at the mercy of a severe lack in internet results for 'Demas Boltof Magic Show'. It was as though they had never existed.

Weeks passed. The front of the heavily shuttered Hidden Dove remained so, even by night, and even when prompted, Nick had no recollection of what had gone on in there. All the while, Harvey couldn't forget Iola. The things he hadn't learnt, and the things he had. A travelling performer would never be easy to find, not unless they came back, but Harvey wouldn't give up, and he refused to forget.

It hadn't just been the way Iola glowed; her talent, her slightly outrageous side; or the passion he had got a glimpse of when she had let her guard down… It was what could have been. The quirks in her personality, rather than the scattering of freckles on her hips: the things he had found when they had spent the night together. Quirks were to be stumbled upon and delighted in, and the glimpse of Iola's had been too palpable to ignore.

Harvey began to wonder if he was in love. He had never felt like this before, and it was more than slightly confusing. Iola's absence intensified what was realistically an infatuation. Harvey had always been too logical, and he understood that he needed to move forward. but it was difficult. He knew Iola hadn't been a dream. She had been real. Felt real. Smelt real...

No magic shows came to the Hidden Dove again. At least, not until long after the first show. Harvey had finished his degree and he was applying for a Masters in music. He played his instruments with enthusiasm; plucked at the Double Bass, combed the guitar with rough fingers and created tuneless but passionate melodies on his keyboard. Iola was painted in the lyrics, entwined in the notes he created.

Then, one day, Nick approached Harvey with a very familiar flyer...

MAGIC SHOW TONIGHT

The Hidden Dove was the venue. Harvey's stomach twisted and his heart simultaneously leapt into his mouth. Never mind that Nick was approaching him in the exact same way he had, half a year ago. *Could be funny.*

They were going, and Harvey was going to find Iola.

*

It was the same again; the derelict façade of the Hidden Dove transformed to a warm, sensual paradise, with a spark and a cheeky wink.

Nick once again got the pints in, and Harvey was vaguely reminded of Groundhog day, until she caught his eye.

The licks of molten gold hair, the far off focus in her eyes, the illegal curve of her hips… She even wore the same dress.

Iola.

Harvey was out of his chair before he could think, and he barely noticed the crash it made as it fell backwards in result of his haste. He was more confident than in their last meeting. Harvey had become a man who knew what he wanted, what he needed, and both of those things were Iola.

If she didn't want him back, then fine, but he would be happy to have his heart broken for trying.

He said her name.

She stopped. She didn't turn.

Harvey began to feel as though something was wrong. The air suddenly felt cold, the club fading from a warm crimson around him to a vile, bright blood scarlet.

'Iola…?'

'How do you know my name?' She asked, in a voice like melting icicles.

Harvey tried to ignore how the hairs on the back of his neck stood to attention. She turned to face him, and there was cold shock in her eyes. 'How did you know?' She faltered on the last word as she looked in Harvey's face; a flicker of recognition passed over it before disappearing.

Harvey was sharp, he didn't miss it.

'Last time you were in Manchester, we...' His face fell as he realised that her hasty façade of failed recognition must be because she regretted their night together. She had regretted meeting him. 'I...' His words shrivelled and died as she glared at him.

'You can't know my name. We've never been to Manchester before.' It seemed her shock was overwhelming what should have been recognition. Impulsive lies bubbling from beneath the surface. Harvey narrowed his eyes.

'Well, you have,' he replied firmly. 'You made this room light up like the Aurora. I remember.'

Iola paled and then, as though they had been anticipating the statement, two men – whom Harvey recognised as some of the 'participants' from the audience in the last show – emerged from the shadows, each taking one of Harvey's arms. Behind them, there was a call of 'oi!' from a very indignant Nick - hands laden with pints - but Harvey was bundled away before he could call back in return.

He was aware of the tight hold on his arms – very aware- and aware that this was certainly not good, and so he struggled, twisting and writhing like an autumn leaf in an updraft.

'You're making this worse,' hissed Iola, who was quite obviously distressed.

The group passed by the curtain and into the wings, despite Harvey desperately digging his heels in, and then they were amongst the small company of magicians... Including Demas.

'I wasn't bothering her,' Harvey objected, twisting and wriggling. 'Honestly. Honestly.'

Demas was hardly made of bravado in the shadows of the back stage. Dark circles, like boats on a river, sat beneath his eyes. His handsome lips were turned down into a foul snarl.

'Who are you?' He demanded, and Harvey blinked in confusion, his eyes constantly flickering to Iola, who stood behind Demas, biting the joint of her index finger.

'I'm just a student. I came to watch your show a few months ago, and-'

'No you didn't. It's impossible!' Demas blustered, his voice becoming slightly more flustered and high pitched. All the while, Iola watched on in concern, and Harvey hung limp in his assailant's grips. 'We'll show you what happens when you step where you shouldn't.' Demas rolled up his sleeves for emphasis. Harvey was certain he heard Iola gasp softly in alarm, anticipating what was to come. 'You certainly won't be able to forget this in the morning…'

The first strike caught his cheek bone – tenderizer to meat – and a cry barely escaped his lips, at least, not until he was released. He lurched forward, and it suddenly seemed as though fists were everywhere; bludgeoning and damaging and rearranging. As Harvey hit the floor, and the first boot struck him, he failed to question if it was worth it: he just knew it had been.

The beating only stopped when the curtain went up.

Harvey would have stayed. Harvey would have asked more questions, but his ribs hurt, and his face certainly didn't feel like his face, and there was blood, swelling and general pain.

It was Nick who found him, and Nick who threatened and swore to anybody near, but nobody listened. They were escorted from the premises in a cloud of anger and confusion - Nick was shoved, Harvey simply staggered. Scorned, they retreated into the night.

'What did you do to deserve that?' Nick asked as they walked and he supported Harvey around his sore shoulders.

'I fell in love, or something,' Harvey murmured in sullen reply.

*

Washing your face thoroughly and peering at yourself in the mirror above the bathroom sink, much like in the movies, was a sure fire way to see how monstrous you looked after a beating. Harvey realised this, some hours later, as the clock struck ten.

It had been a ridiculous night. Indeed, it had been a ridiculous few months. It had taken time to get rid of overprotective Nick so that Harvey could wallow alone, and even more time for him to wash, and realise just how bizarre everything had become. It was as though he was in his own weird version of 'Round the Twist' and that wasn't a particularly appealing notion.

The doorbell rang. Harvey moved through the grotty halls of his student house, finally hesitating at the front door. He looked a mess. It was late. His attackers hadn't found him, had they? Come back to knock another seven bells into him with meaty fists and heavy set boots?

'Who is it?' He called warily through the door. There was a brief silence, and then-

'It's not Demas.'

Harvey dragged the door open. It shuddered and rattled in its hinges.

On the door step, clad in a pea green rain coat, was Iola. She regarded his injuries with obvious guilt.

'I thought I'd come by,' she said. 'You're the only one who's ever remembered.'

There was a silence between them. Harvey didn't consider inviting her inside.

'I thought it was a good show,' he replied, with little enthusiasm.

'You're not supposed to know that,' Iola smiled, but it was sad; a knowing smile that craved for a break in monotony. Harvey recognised it all too well. 'You're supposed to forget.'

Harvey looked confused.

'I wasn't about to forget you in a hurry.'

Iola's cheeks went pink; an entirely different reaction to the first compliment Harvey had given her. He noticed how she made no attempt to apologise about the kicking he had received. He didn't question why.

'The show stays the same, and so do the audience,' Iola explained. 'It's a cheat, but Demas has been at it for years.'

Harvey thought briefly about the inconsistencies in his research on the travelling show and he considered the huge gaps in Nick's memory. What had seemed like drunken dents in perception, suddenly became forced failures.

The night was cold and smelt of ice, but Harvey still made no move to offer Iola the warmth of his home. It was the first time she had spoken to him without prompt.

'You should know,' she began, and Harvey considered interrupting, demanding why… Again, he didn't. 'You just should.' She hesitated. 'We've had the same audience for years. They never remember the show, Harvey. That's the game. Make them forget, gain a captive audience. Sure fire money from people who will always attend.' She shrugged. 'Real magicians, like us, really struggle for work. The false have the monopoly.'

Harvey didn't consider how ridiculous the statement 'real magicians' was, because it almost made sense. Of course Iola hadn't been normal.

'Con artists,' he said. 'Real, magical…' Iola shrugged in reply. 'Look,' Harvey went on, 'I don't know why you came here. I spent all that time looking for you, and I've got a fat lip and a cracked rib to show for it. I know it was stupid, but I remembered you, and I wanted to take that chance.' He held her gaze, earnest and hurt, and Iola's expression crumpled, just slightly, before she raised her arm. Harvey watched, hand on the door, ready, but not quite able to close it.

From the cuff of her pea green sleeve, Iola produced a key. A very familiar key. Harvey's old house key. She demonstrated it with a smile, and then it disappeared in her hand, before reappearing out of the opposite sleeve. Harvey managed a delighted chuckle, and took the key as she held it out to him.

'You kept it,' he said, quite surprised and pleased.

Iola's eyes remained level with his.

'I didn't forget, either.'

Suburbia

I feel I must make one thing absolutely clear, right now, at the start of this... this... Well, testimony, I suppose, is the only word for it now – since the truth has come out. The truth about what happened in that neighbourhood, all those years ago...

You have to understand, this story may seem to be a lot of things, but the one thing that I *am* certain of – and the one thing that kept me from recounting it sooner, laying all this to rest – is that the cold-bloodedness I encountered that awful day is proof of the grotesque side of humanity; the side that can live in plain sight, masquerading as normalcy... The side that made me run and hide, afraid that it would follow me, find me – and that no one would believe my story.

But the past is always dug up, isn't it? And now the papers have discovered the truth, I feel I can keep silent no longer.

It was January; one that was cool and crisp, without too much heavy rain and a chilling wind that seemed to catch you with its stinging, whipping grasp the second you stepped outside. Due to my job as an on-call electrician, I stepped into its path quite a lot, although once the first couple of clients were out of the way, I was usually growing used to the numbing spread of biting cold that gnawed at me, even despite my thick, uniform jacket.

This particular January, I remember vividly, was the scene of a mounting economic recession, a word that was thrown out into the face of the public so many times that one began to feel as if there had never been anything before the downturn. Money was tight, but then for many it always had been and I was no exception.

It was mid-morning when I arrived at the address listed. The neighbourhood itself was nothing out of the ordinary. It presented itself as an unimposing, regular little circulation of modern, semi-detached houses, so completely indistinguishable from any other district that it caught me off guard. The residents there at the time of my horrific visit, those that chilled me to the bone quicker than even a full-blown gale of that January wind, are gone now, of course. Discovered and brought to justice themselves finally.

I rang the bell of the attractively modern detached house that loomed centrally above its neighbours in the area and waited, kit in hand, naively admiring the neat order of the garden and the building's solid frame, similar to the others around it. When the door opened, I was met with a middle-aged, gracious woman, whose dark blonde hair was short and perfectly curled, her whole appearance immediately discerning her as one whom, whilst having a pleasant, welcoming face, liked everything to be done properly and in order.

Once inside, Mrs Adams asked me if I would like a cup of tea; I politely declined. I'd had three 'courtesy cups', as I called them, already. Her house was as pristine inside as she was, everything typically beige, muted and well-ordered; very middle-class "keeping up appearances".

There was a funny smell though, one that lingered everywhere, despite the numerous pots of potpourri studding the polished surfaces. It even overwhelmed Mrs Adams' own powerful brand of sickly perfume. I couldn't quite put my finger on what that odour was at the time - it was the smell of something charred, but not the same as when wood or food smells when burnt... It mingled with this sort of... wet, fleshy, overwhelming scent, like burning fruit pulp or vegetable fat. The smell wafted down from the upper storeys and was deeply unpleasant; I tried to rearrange my expression into something carefully neutral at exactly the same time as trying to work out what on earth could have caused such an intense stench to permeate the entire house. It was almost like it had seeped into the furnishings and the walls over time...

If Mrs Adams noticed my discomfort, it didn't show; she remained just as professionally neutral as I was attempting to. Smiling brightly, she warmly asked how long I had worked for the electric company. Her tone was remarkably cordial, affable and sociable, which surprised me somewhat, not least because I was partly distracted by that bizarre smell. Most customers preferred me to check the meter, or fix whichever problem had called me there, and then head out as quickly as possible – and, I must confess, upon perceiving her at the front door, I had instantly assumed that she would be one of those clients rather... unnerving in their attitude.

148

At the time though, *unnerving* meant nothing more than that she was sure to view me as an interruption to her day – I appreciate the irony, now that I look back.

'And I'm sure your client numbers must have increased, what with the 'Recession',' She was still talking, all but whispering the last word and entitling it with a roguish capital that made it seem even more important. 'I'm sure everyone must be calling you out with queries into how they can save their money.'

'Oh, yes, well,' I began, but had barely uttered anything more when there was a loud, chilling shriek from somewhere upstairs in the house, a distant echo to its sound that suggested it came from above even the second floor. I started violently and turned hastily towards Mrs Adams, afraid that there was some member of her family in need of help, or... Well, I didn't know what.

Mrs Adams merely smiled at the look of startled alarm on my face and nodded her head in the direction of the ceiling.

'My husband and some of our friends from the neighbourhood.' Her voice was full of gaiety and it threw me — the whole situation threw me, I had no idea what she meant. I must have expressed that in some subconscious way, losing my careful neutrality, for a moment later she elaborated. 'We converted our attic – it was always rather spacious, you see. So now, every week or so, we can all meet together and have a little hearing.'

I nodded dumbly, casting another dubious look at the staircase. I was nonplussed as to what she

149

was referring to and, for the life of me, couldn't fathom why someone would be wailing like that during what she seemed to be suggesting was some sort of Neighbourhood Watch gathering. She cheerfully beckoned me out of the sitting room and towards the kitchen. Maybe they were some sort of amateur dramatic society; she could have been referring to that. Yes, I decided, that must be it. What else could it be?

What else could it be indeed?

'Mr Finlow, from down the street,' she continued, as she motioned me to follow her along the hallway, 'He's an incredibly good handyman – fixed us up with two good sturdy chairs and *very* safely wired circuits.'

Uncertain as I was of where the chairs fitted in, her mention of circuits seemed to reinforce my ideas of the theatrical, odd as the whole notion still was. Whoever heard of an am-dram theatre in an attic? However, eccentricity, as I considered it at that early moment, is a funny thing; you never know where it's going to manifest itself.

I was still musing on this when I noticed some subtle marring of her beautifully pristine interior decoration. The hallway, which was long and thin, led from the front door down to the kitchen; the dark wooden staircase stretched upwards along one side and doorways to the sitting room and dining room branched off on the right. It was just past the stairs that I noticed it; along the upper reaches of the wall, streaking through the fawn coloured paint, were sets of continuous scratches, four in a row - they ripped and flaked the paint and paper jaggedly, and stretched across a good couple of feet.

It looked for all the world like fingernail marks...

Or they could have just been moving a piece of heavy furniture recently, tipped at an awkward angle. I knew well enough how those sorts of repair jobs were usually the last to be dealt with. But even so... The smell, the scream, now this? I repressed a shudder.

Mrs Adams brought me out of my reverie by gesturing to a door in the corner of the spacious kitchen, one that clearly led down to a cellar or storeroom. She opened her mouth to speak, but was cut off by the sound of loud, desperate, terrified weeping drifting down in the wake of the shriek. I stared at her; she pressed a hand against the chunky pearl necklace that sat on her collarbone. For a moment she tapped the beads with long fingernails, giving me a wide, expounding smile, before inclining her head towards the door.

'Shall we continue down? That's where the meter is.' She elegantly led the way forward, descending the stairs gracefully. As I moved to follow, a pleading voice reverberated down, high-pitched and loud:

'No! Please, *no*!'

Now, you must understand, I had been on the job a good while, young as I then was, and I had seen many an odd person – homes overrun with cats, dogs, parrots, whole menageries of variously assorted animals. I've met brattish children who seem to run the home, obscure modern painters, people who only decorate their house in one shade of colour... I once even entered in on the W.I during their charity 'Calendar Girls' photo shoot. After that experience, I found little else capable to shock me.

But this house, this day... It seemed odd in a way that was instinctive and unexplainable to me, at least at the time. My nerves were on edge, my heart pounding; I could taste the metallic tang of adrenaline at the back of my throat as I followed that inscrutable woman to the cellar door.

Still under the impression that they were an amateur theatre company, I felt that – partly out of a polite curiosity and partly to rid myself of that incessant nervousness – I should enquire into the matter a little. So, choosing the most obvious of questions, I remarked, 'I take it you *are* a drama society? You must be rehearsing something pretty tragic – Hamlet?'

We had reached the bottom of the stairs and she stood back to let me access the electricity meter. It was just as I had placed my kit on the ground beside me, peering at the screen of the meter, straining my eyes through the dim light that was shed by the bare bulb dangling from the ceiling, that she let forth an incredibly amused, chiming laugh.

'Oh, dear me, no – we're not the neighbourhood amateur dramatics. We just take care of a few of the indiscretions that occur, often with the more difficult tenants in the estate.'

My original neighbourhood watch thoughts drifted back to me... And the noises I had previously heard - the strange smell and the scratches - suddenly became more sinister.

I tried to shrug it off.

'I see. So you...' I left the question open, although to this day I am not sure why. I see now, as I have done since that dreadful moment of realisation, that I should have just dropped the conversation there and then, and hastened to get the hell out of there. But I was young; I had seen plenty of strange things... And who would ever believe that such terrible cold-bloodedness could cross their path as easily as you'd cross a gypsy's palm with silver? There's no smoke without fire, sure – but I didn't want to spark the embers without provocation, no matter how strange the situation had become.

I always look back with pride at that moment of trusting, youthful innocence. And then I always curse my younger self for the fool that I was.

'Oh, you know how it is...' Mrs Adams smiled primly – a bone-chilling smile, one that haunts me still. 'People who arrive in the neighbourhood, or have been here for years, and are merely nothing more than difficult, stubborn mules, until one day – *snap!* They push the boundaries too far. So, naturally, they have to be dealt with by the community in a fair, hard-handed manner. We meet here, bring the guilty party along and come to a decision.'

'I see,' I said again.

Except I didn't see – I didn't see at all.

Pausing from my inspection of the meter, I turned to look at her and, for the first time, took in the basement as well. What had initially seemed like shadowy junk slid into focus beneath the penumbra cast from the light bulb; some sort of bizarre office, hidden away at the bottom of the house. There were boxes stacked haphazardly against the only remaining wall, flyers and papers overflowing in bundles and loose folders - newspaper articles, reports, photographs clearly going back months, maybe even years... Across from me, mounted on another wall, was a huge notice board – like the ones in police dramas on TV – only this one seemed possessed of a far more sinister purpose in the shifty cellar of the Adams' home.

It was covered with a home-drawn map of the neighbourhood; around each house depicted were photographs, stalker-snapshots of couples kissing, a man walking a dog, two children dropping a sweet wrapper into the gutter... Circles, crosses, red markings dotted these and other clippings surrounding the map – worse still were the photos beneath, laid out neatly in a row: headshots of desperate looking men and women, all with a date below... A strange suburban collection of increasingly horrifying menace.

For a long, elastic moment I fought against the beads of perspiration dewing across my forehead - this had to be a joke. I had heard of such practical pranks being played by oddities in the general public before, on some fellow unsuspecting colleagues. Surely this was one of them?

Just one big laugh at the expense of the "staff", the working stiff... Right?

Hindsight is a terrible, terrible thing.

Swallowing, waiting for the raucous laughter - perhaps even the hidden camera - I slowly refocused my attention on Mrs Adams, who was watching me with the same placid smile, the same long-nailed finger tap-tap-tapping away at her peals. As I phrased my next question, I will never forget the look on her face as she received it, nor the one that immediately followed as she answered.

'So... you *are* like a neighbourhood watch group? You mean that you... revoke inconsiderate residents' privileges, stop their free parking or involvement in community matters; things like that?'

Her pealing laugh sounded again, her face both grotesquely shadowed and illuminated by halves in the muted light of the maniacally littered basement. A gleam of hungry, self-righteous belief flickered in her greying eyes.

'Oh no, dear: the more serious the crime, the more serious the punishment - and we make sure to update our methods regularly, to keep our standards at the absolute highest level. Last week, Mrs Chalters was found to be sleeping with the local butcher – very disagreeable that was, a complete *scandal*. That sort of impropriety and blatant adultery cannot go unnoticed, you know, it would have been a disgrace to our established, *caring* neighbourhood. They've both been dealt with now though, of course.'

'Really?' I managed to faintly reply. The sheer absurdity and ruthlessness of it clings to the back of my conscious mind constantly – the vision of the basement, the dawning horror of the charred, fleshy smell and those scraping nail marks.... The only way to evade their scarring, clawing grip on my dreams, on my nightmares, was to run away and never spoke these words out loud. To think of the

155

insanity that lurks in some people, the complete monstrosity that can be brought out by one trivial little circumstance is a thought that cannot be suppressed, once the realisation has dawned. People simply won't believe it – until they have to. I sure as hell didn't want to believe it myself.

'Oh yes,' Mrs Adams eagerly continued. 'Mr Chalters was most pleased with the speed and professionalism with which we reached a verdict. We actually have another case today, right at this very moment, with the jury all assembled to hear the final motion.'

'Jury?' I was quite breathless by this point, dizzy with all the ghastly scenarios being placed before me. I had, through no fault of my own, stumbled into a nest of madmen.

'Yes, yes – judge, jury... and the executioner, of course.'

I felt my blood curdle and my stomach drop heavily. I was frozen to the spot, still desperate for this to be some cruel prank, a joke at my expense to entertain the family - even the entire nation, I wouldn't have cared at that point, abject humiliation or not...

Anything was better than that terrible, yawning truth.

'Ex-executioner?'

'Of course. The Lorrimers are under a very serious charge; their dog has been befouling the driveways and gardens of this neighbourhood for months and months now. But they never did a thing to stop the little brute running free and acting as it chooses, despite our numerous warnings. But the jury's out now – they should have listened sooner.'

'But… I mean, how can you possibly execu–' As though some ironic twist of fate had heard the prefix to my stammering question, a hideous scream sounded from the attic, a fearful, hair-raising, spine-tingling, absolutely pain-filled human scream, one that made my flesh crawl and to this day haunts my every waking nightmare, catching me when I am most off my guard. I clearly recall how rapidly the light above my head flickered and hummed, blinking on and off every millisecond.

Then, shockingly abrupt, the scream died to a sharp halt, silence ensuing. The light wavered once more and then pinged back to its usual life, illuminating both Mrs Adams and myself with a new clarity, both of us gazing at the ceiling, an expression of satisfaction lining her face and one, I have no doubt, of complete terror on mine. In that startlingly hushed moment, the meaning of her previous words rang out to me as clear as a bell tolling.

Confirmation of the origins of that hideous smell soon followed, seeping into my brain with a clarity so intense that I thought I might vomit.

Clapping her hands, she settled herself in my direction once more, businesslike.

'Well, the motion was carried!' My eyes slowly fell on her calm, fulfilled countenance, utterly horrified beyond words. I feel, in these long-growing days of my later life, that that woman will forever be a spectre looming over me, the embodiment of the ills of society that I see and hear about every day. 'I do so like to see good justice carried out swiftly and fittingly. I should have been there to see the motion through myself, you know, but as this was the only day your company could 'slot us in', we felt it would be necessary to take the appointment – beneficial, in the long run, too.'

I was numb with the terrible vileness of it all, shocked to the very core. I felt as though I could barely breathe; a visceral heaviness seemed to have descended upon me, preventing me from movement, from feeling, from everything except that terrible comprehension. The scream rang in my ears and my stomach heaved. Mrs Adams watched me expectantly, her hands folded in front of her. Finally, after what felt like a long, dreadful age had passed, I managed to murmur indistinctly, 'what do you mean, beneficial?'

'Well,' she replied, looking somewhat surprised. 'We called you out so that we could obtain some advice. -- We're looking to keep our bill down.'

Jessica's Wise and Future Self

I finished packing the last box – filled to the brim with yellowing books, annuals and old records that might serve well in a charity shop window.

I'd had the option, of course, to keep whatever I wanted of Granddad's things – but aside from the bizarre Austrian cuckoo clock that had familiarly hung over the fireplace for so many years, I'd decided against it; too many memories.

I folded the box flaps in on themselves - fitting them together like a jigsaw – and wiped a stray tear from my eye. I straightened up and regarded the house around me, realising for the first time that this was it, that the house would truly remain empty; at least while it waited to go up for auction.

It still smelled like Granddad, though.

The once full-of-life kitchen had been reduced to empty units; counters once graced with sweets and cakes of equally fattening shapes and sizes stood quiet and white, severely lacking the companionship of a full tea pot. I remembered, with a heart that both clenched and soared, that when I was smaller, Granddad would let me put extra sprinkles on the cakes, or pick the mugs I liked best for the next round of tea. I had felt so important –

reaching up on tiptoes, pointing to the brightest colours I could, and in most cases, the floweriest of the patterns.

The last time I had done that had been the year before. Now fully grown – a woman with my own home – Granddad had prompted me to add sprinkles to the Victoria Sponge, and I had done so with glee, before pulling down the flowery mugs myself with a giggle.

I released a sigh and gathered the heavy box in both arms, heading back out to meet my waiting mother. My shoes thudded loudly on the bare wooden floor – reminding me boisterously of the emptiness. My attention was drawn to the curtain-less windows, like eyes without lids... The vacant book shelves, hungry cabinets and lonely chairs waiting to be removed by professionals in the coming week.

The house's personality had been snatched, and a lump formed itself in my throat as I shoved the box on the back seat of the car, and slid into the driver's seat beside mum.

The engine revved over her question of 'are you alright?' and my crisp lie unfurled as we reversed out of the drive.

'I'm fine.'

*

Of course, it wouldn't be incorrect to assume that I was not at all fine.

Granddad's cuckoo clock watched me with amusement from its place above the fireplace, but I mostly ignored it as I trailed back and forth, impatiently taking part in a phone call with my sister.

'It's all packed up. I'm fine about it,' I insisted, crossing the small lounge of the flat, passing the window sill and its proud display of photo frames - many of which featured Granddad. Birthday after birthday, graduation, walks in the sun, holidays… He had always been there.

Perhaps that was the worst part.

'The more you tell people you're fine, the more they think the opposite.' Eva replied, and I rolled my eyes and prodded the corpse of a fallen sock with my toe.

'Well, that's a silly view to have, isn't it?' Came my curt reply, and an exasperated growl was her answer.

'Don't tell me you're still hanging about on your own, Jess.'

'No,' I lied, again, and I gestured to the flat, though the act was pointless, as there was no-one to see it - no-one aside from my cat Bosley, who watched lazily from the arm of the sofa. 'I've got plenty of company.'

'Your cat doesn't count,' said Eva, and my hand clenched over her phone. 'Look, it's been months. Come out with me and the girls tonight. We'll have cocktails, go for a dance…'

My gaze roamed, trying to focus on anything that would distract me, and it only fixated on the stack of Granddad's old letters I'd been sorting through. Again, my heart gave an unhealthy clench – another attempt to tear itself apart with grief – and I bit down on my lip to stifle a sob.

'Okay,' I managed, in an effort to finish the conversation before the tears really began to pour, 'text me.'

I hung up abruptly and, once again, anguish overwhelmed me. It sealed all other emotions away and overran my mind, forcing me onto the sofa and into a heap of juddering sobs. I had been hoping, as each day woke me, that it would get easier. That time would fix me. It hadn't. If anything, it had only become harder.

What did Eva understand? She had never been half as interested in Granddad as I had. She had never understood our wonderful companionship, and she never would.

I remembered one Autumn morning in October, during the school holidays. Reminiscing on his RAF days, Granddad had suggested we go together to watch the planes fly out from the airport. He had always enjoyed the modernised metal monsters, and despite being a little girl who adored all manner of typically feminine things – horses with wild, beautiful manes, all shades of pink, perfumes – I had leapt at the chance to watch the planes with Granddad.

I'd have leapt at the chance to go anywhere with him. All the while, however, Eva had sat by us with her arms folded, sulkily declaring that it was 'boring'.

She had never understood.

Still, she had a point, annoyingly. I had become something of a recluse, deciding I much preferred the company of the television, and Bosley, so as a result, those were the two things that always greeted me when I arrived home. No long term boyfriend, no chatty phone call. Just emptiness.

Grief wasn't attractive on me.

That much was proven, several hours later, when I got a good look at myself in the bathroom mirror, ready to smother my face in all manner of makeup for my first night out in a long time. The tantalising hazel of my eyes had become pastel – cold and sad. They were the most obvious sign of my hurt, amongst black curls on caramel skin. I'd have to work above and beyond to fix this.

I just couldn't believe how others coped with the cruel reality of death; the constant of absence... the jabbing reminder that you really, truly were not going to get that person back. It was terribly unfair, and it seemed almost impossible that the hole would remain gaping; that it would never close.

How was death so common, so...accepted?

Perhaps anyone's first experience of death was like this, I reasoned as I stared at the outfit I had laid out for the evening. I thought about just how much I didn't want to go out, and resented the clothes for it. Things would have to get easier at some point.

I just wished it would happen sooner.

*

The night out with Eva and her friends was a veritable nightmare. In an effort to avoid the elephant in the room, pitchers of cocktails had been

164

ordered in, which were drunk from straws while I was questioned relentlessly about 'men on the scene'. It was as though there was nothing else to question in my life, as if the lack of a significant other was the height of interest. I had answered as best as I could, but there wasn't much to say.

How could I say that I lacked the motivation to do anything? That the washing up was a teetering tower and social invitations had become so few and far between that the comedy channels were more acquainted with me?

While I was aware of how different I had become to my normal, eager self, I didn't feel ready to change. Not yet.

I had told myself this every day since Granddad had died - convinced myself it was temporary when it was looking less so by the day.

I considered all of this as I slipped off my heeled shoes and massaged my aching feet. It was only 10pm - hardly a night out, but then again, I had been no fun anyway.

I slumped on the edge of the unmade bed - I never seemed to find the time to make it anymore. Life had become monotonous as I tried to understand and cope with my loss. I was daytime television - repeating myself day in, day out. A lifestyle once smattered with lunch dates, weekends away and days in the city had dimmed to lonely routine. Wake up, grieve. Work, grieve. Eat, grieve. Bed, grieve. Grieve, grieve, grieve.

Except for today.

Today, something went 'thump'.

Tears trembled down my cheeks - I shed so many now I barely noticed the beginning, anymore - and I wiped them away absently as I searched for the source of the noise.

It had been a whisper of a sound - something hitting something so softly it could have been placed down with human hands. Bemused, I looked around, and almost immediately my gaze settled on the bedside table... and the passport resting lazily atop it.

Considering I hadn't been out of the country in at least two years, this struck me as odd, and taking into account that the only thing on said bedside table as of late had been the final Harry Potter book - which the passport now sat upon - it struck me as absolutely one hundred per cent Twilight-Zone odd.

I took it in hand, noting how battered it was – slightly bent and tatty, but evidently used and loved. Last time I had seen it, my own passport had looked nothing like that. I flipped to the back page to get a look at my thoroughly unattractive passport photo, and uncovered my slightly chubby twenty year old self staring back at me with eyes of one severely hung over.

The next thing I found made my heart double in pace.

Well before the hard plastic back page, my fingers paused in their rapid flicking of the pages so that I could focus on the middle spread.

Two stamps, one on each page – side by side like frames on a wall – proudly declared themselves as entry and exit to Bangladesh. I scratched my head. I had certainly never been to Bangladesh. I had never even left the EU. My brain rattled around in confusion, until it noticed the next bizarre revelation.

The dates.

I had apparently arrived in Bangladesh on February 14th 2015. Over a year on from now. The second stamp informed me of my leaving, three weeks after that.

My eyes desperately searched for more information, while my mind reeled through explanations like negative camera film.

Was this a joke? I couldn't imagine Eva, or any one of my estranged friends playing a joke on me in my current emotional state. Ironically, it was something Granddad would have done. The twang of hurt at the thought was almost instantly stifled with curiosity. If this was a carefully choreographed joke, it didn't explain how the passport had gently thudded into existence on my copy of Harry Potter and the Deathly Hallows.

Apart from the well-used state of the passport, it was certainly mine. It even boasted the same smudge of nail varnish I had spilt on its burgundy cover the night before a university trip to France. I flipped to the front. I had been to Australia, apparently. Two months were spent there... Or were going to be, in the spring of 2014.

My fingers became a quivering blur – scraping through page after page – the next two years of my life mapped out and displayed in stamp form, like a bizarre collector's book. Thailand to

China, China to Bangladesh, Bangladesh to Egypt, to Morocco, to Russia, to Canada, to America...

Except none of it had happened yet.

Thrilled to have something so fascinating and something to take the edge off my mood – I slid off the bed in search of my own passport. It took scrabbling through several drawers, and the upending of a few unlucky ones before I found the item in question. I took off back to the bedroom, frightening Bosley on the way and laid the two passports side by side.

The older, more used one was definitely the same. Every element was identical... It was only time that separated them. I wished I could have made sense of it. I wanted it to be a joke – because how else was this bizarre happenstance reality? The facts rolled around in my head like snooker balls. Nobody I knew would go to this effort to trick me. Nobody would dare, yet I was sitting there, believing more so in the possibility of time travel than anything else. It made no sense. It was utterly absurd. This wasn't an HG Wells novel, things like this just didn't happen, and contrary to what may have been going on behind the closed doors of science – time travel certainly didn't exist.

What would Granddad have thought?

For the first time in so long, I smiled at the memory of him. At the thought of his amused shrug and that well-travelled and all-knowing incline of his head. *You're losing it, Jessie. You're madder than me!*

Tickled, and for once, happily reminiscent of Granddad, I opened my own passport; my present one.

No stamps.

Not a one.

The sight was far more disappointing than I had anticipated, even though I had already known the outcome. No medals of honour for the unadventurous. I would have been okay with that before Granddad had passed away, but now that I had seen the blank pages of the present passport, compared with the vibrant, smiling stamped ones of the future, I felt exposed and afraid.

The realisation made me feel as though I was teetering on a see-saw, dipping and resurfacing – and I knew right there, that regardless of why, or how this passport had ended up on my bedside table, wrinkled and loved, I had to honour it.

For me, and of course, for Granddad.

*

Just under a year later, I was at the airport, loaded up with bags, confidence and love. Eva and Mum had come to wave me off, and they watched me with trepidation – as though they were seeing Bambi step out onto the ice.

'This is your last chance, Jessica. You can still come home.' Mum's eyebrows were knitted into an all too familiar frown, which I tried to extinguish with a smile.

'It's a bit late now. I'm scared, yes, but I was far more scared before this.'

'We should just be glad she's leaving her flat, mum. Bosley's had a lucky escape,' Eva said good humouredly, giving me a wink. It was too true for an argument.

The past year had been hard – almost more than the immediate aftermath of the clearance of Granddad's house. I had enthusiastically broken into years' worth of savings for my travels, and the rest had been planning and saving, planning… and saving some more. I'd even taken on extra shifts at work to cover my bills in the meantime. The passport from the future had watched me knowingly from my bookshelf, giving me support as much as photos and letters from Granddad had. Slowly but surely, I had stepped into the metaphorical sunshine, and winced at how difficult the journey so far had been.

Now I would say goodbye to my family for the next few years and hello to myself.

*

Australia

I tried not to think about where the passport was leading me and why. I could only hope that my future self wouldn't have sent me the passport for anything but a good reason.

I began to care less and less about the motives of the Jessica I didn't know yet as I stepped onto the white sand of Cottesloe Beach in Western Australia.

170

I had my sandals in one hand, teetering from my fingers as I strolled. It was approaching sunset, and crowds were already gathering to stare out at the blue expanse of Indian Ocean; waiting for magic.

Already, my head felt clearer. It was an amalgamation of the foreign sand between my toes, the distinct scent of adventure in the humid air... and the view wasn't bad, either.

The beach itself had been recommended to me by a local and so, keen to throw myself into my adventure with enthusiasm, I had made Cottesloe my first stop as the night drew in.

While busy and not exactly private, the beach held a charm that made me feel I had my own special connection to it, despite sharing the sand with hundreds of others. The sea crept forward, and over it, like pink flames licking at the heavens, was dusk. The sun hung low like a medallion - oddly reminiscent to me of Granddad's commemorative armed forces badge, presented to him by the Queen. I remembered with a fond tear in my eye, that he had displayed it proudly – bringing it up whenever the conversation steered remotely close to his past, and even when it didn't. I had loved his pride, and it had been something that had rubbed off on me, too. While it had made me a force to be reckoned with at one time, it also made me closer to Granddad.

The sun sank lower, painting lazy shadows over the beach, dashing hues of oranges, blues and finally purples over the sky: its very own canvas above. My eyes danced as I watched, entirely certain that I had never seen or experienced anything more beautiful.

I thanked myself for Australia; no longer a possibility in my future, but a certainty in my present.

*

Bangladesh

I had planned my trip around the world to the point of an obsessive compulsive, but it was worth it. Each country or city had something separate I wanted to experience; for Bangladesh, I had hired a tour guide to save me from bumbling down the heaving colony of streets in the city.

Her name was Amala, and she was already my favourite person. I was more than thankful for her and the companionship. Together, we traversed the food markets India had to offer, and eventually ended up just outside Srimongal, where Amala introduced me to Seven Layer Tea. I had jumped at the chance to visit the tea capital of Bangladesh, and I wasn't disappointed.

I won't forget the humid day we spent in Nilkhantha Tea Cabin, drinking syrupy tea, striped in glasses that proudly displayed seven shades of rich browns ranging from coffee to toffee. Waves of flavour washed over my tongue, teasing me with cinnamon and the bitter tang of black and green teas. It was deliciously detached from anything I could have consumed back home, and it gave me confidence.

'Have you ever lost anyone?' I asked Amala suddenly, watching as her dark eyes flicked to mine questioningly. We had been getting on wonderfully – we shared passions and opinions, but now the conversation juddered awkwardly.

'Yes,' Amala said finally, 'my dog, actually. Just recently.' She shook her head, and smiled sadly. 'My best friend. Why?'

I almost wished I hadn't brought it up. There was hurt, there, but I ploughed on, sipping the tea to empower me.

'How did you cope?'

Amala swallowed some of her own tea and I got the impression that she was using it for the same reason as I had.

'I did not,' she explained. 'Not at first. But I made sure I never felt bad about the grieving process.' She span her glass around distractedly in both hands. 'My favourite writer, J.R.R. Tolkein once said: 'do not weep, for not all tears are an evil', and I believe that to be true.'

For a moment, I was struck by Amala's earnest reply, and tears sprung to my eyes as the words hit me. I wanted to tell her why I had come and why I was alone, but how could I explain about the passport and the fear it had induced of a life going unlived? I could feel it burning in my backpack – watching me with its knowing eyes. It was an unnerving thing to have around, something so weighed down with knowledge of my future. While I had got used to its presence, the moments I really considered it sent shivers down my spine.

I couldn't say anything, and so I finished my tea, letting it soothe me. Amala was regarding me with obvious worry and discomfort. I cut her off before she could comment.

'You're right,' I said with an assured smile. 'Thank you.'

Noticing that she too had finished, I rubbed my hands together eagerly. 'So, what can we try next?'

*

All of the countries I visited were memorable. The passport took me to corners of the world I would have never known to exist, and each time the little blank book received a stamp, I swelled with pride.

I travelled to Russia in winter – most specifically Moscow, which was a city iced in snow, blazing bleach white.

I traversed the flat terrain of Egypt - stared at the Pyramids that reached the sky, sampled delicacies and made friends in the hotel bar.

I watched over the manmade Rice Terraces of Yuanyang, China – a place lacking in tourism but rich in beauty and ethnic minorities. I was struck by the sense of community there, and the sight itself of the rice fields - lips of settlements trailing down hills like steps to a giant's haven.

Morocco frightened me, but in ways that made me grow. The streets were full of intense poverty, but the markets were a thing to behold – made up of rich colours that set my eyes alight.

It was only certain nights when I remembered my loss. Those dark times were unavoidable; they closed in on me with sharp claws of anxiety and pain, puncturing my new found veil of confidence until it was left torn and tattered. Only when the sun rose again, did it heal.

*

America

The great form of the Lincoln Memorial watched me imposingly from his throne of marble, and I sat on the steps, my attentions focused on the length of pool opposite. It reflected the clusters of tourists standing at its perimeter, snapping away with oversized cameras. I ruminated there, tuning out the humming background noise of traffic and people.

I was on the last leg of my travels and it was an odd feeling – almost like a new loss. It was there, that for the first time in a while, that I thought about Granddad, and with a surprising finality, too.

There had been a time when I couldn't have thought of him in the past tense; it was too hard – it made my heart and my head hurt. Now it came easily. I wasn't sure I liked it… but I had let it happen. I was surprisingly okay with the realisation. It had been so long, such a vast adventure. I had grown like a thriving plant, reaching for the stars, standing tall, healthy and beaming. My past self was a shadow and I was the light.

I took out a pen and a wad of post cards. It seemed like a pivotal moment, and a fitting location for it. Amala would be first – we had hit it off, and I had promised to keep her updated on all of my adventures. On the reverse of a cheesy collage of Washington landmarks, I began to scribble… only to be interrupted.

'Do you mind if I borrow your pen once you're done?'

I looked up and caught the gaze of a man who was more 'touristy' than me – if that was possible. His t-shirt declared him a visitor to Niagara falls, and his smile flattered his playfully bright eyes. In one hand, he held an even bigger bundle of post cards than I had. I couldn't help but laugh.

'Ah, you have a waiting audience, too?'

I was surprised at how smooth and confident my reply was, though I suppose I shouldn't have been, in wake of the changes I had made.

'Is it that obvious?' Came the amused reply, and I recognised his English accent immediately – Londoner.

I giggled and fished about in my bag, muttering 'actually', before producing another pen entirely. He looked impressed and took it with thanks. Together, we sat in the sun and wrote to our loved ones.

A conversation soon began, wherein we discussed and described who each recipient was to us, and why. We learnt an awful lot about one another in that hour, sun soaked and bright with holiday giddiness. By the end of the talk, we knew one another's best friends, siblings and parents by name.

'Yours is about the only name I don't know,' he pointed out, and I let out a faux gasp of horror.

'How awful of me. It's Jessica.'

'And I'm Matthew.'

We shook hands. The touch lingered. Matthew licked his lips hesitantly. 'Perhaps I could add you to my postcard list?'

*

Matthew and I ended up travelling the USA together. We were inseparable. Before the trip, I would have questioned how easily such a thing could have happened, but the same could have been blustered by someone who had never fallen in love.

We ate s'mores by a campfire in Yellowstone National Park, kissed by the edge of the Grand Canyon and revisited our childhoods in Universal Studios.

We found ourselves hiking through Yosemite Valley in California, surrounded by monoliths – proud and commanding over-sized teeth of granite, which waited to consume us in their jaws. High brush strokes of green made up the surrounding sequoia trees and as Matthew and I walked hand in hand, I reflected that this was more like a fantasy – one I had stepped into by luck alone.

Perhaps it was the amazing and beautiful surroundings, the crooked chasms of rock and the watching lake. Perhaps it was the serenity –

reminiscent of Granddad... but it was there that I finally confided my loss, and the story of the passport... all to Matthew.

Together, we sat amongst the trees and I showed him both – now nearly identical; equally battered and stamped alike, apart from one - the leaving stamp for America. In a week, I would gain that, too. One was a totem of the future, and the other... my present. I could scarcely tell the difference in the two passports any more. It was refreshing.

Matthew turned each tiny book over and over in his hands, looking puzzled. He was evidently unsure what to think. I didn't feel nervous – I had come to accept them for what they were, regardless of where they came from, or how, or why... I knew I was at peace with that.

'What happens when you get the last stamp? What do you do?' Matthew tapped the empty page of my present passport, balancing it on his lap beside the other one for comparison. I frowned and leaned in.

'I hadn't thought of that,' I said honestly, feeling suddenly exposed. How was I supposed to get it back? Time travel hadn't been invented, and wasn't necessarily possible. What was I supposed to do? My past self needed it! I tried to articulate my words again, but all I could manage was 'I...'

A warm hand was on my cheek in a moment, and soft, loving lips pressed to mine; Mathew, so supportive, even of who he must have perceived to be a mad woman.

'You got this far,' he soothed, once he had pulled away, 'You can go further still.'

Warm hope and love flooded in my veins.

He was right.

*

Home

I expected all of the grief to come roaring back when I touched down in England for the first time in two years. I expected to relapse, even though I had grown so much…

But I didn't.

Even when I set foot in my flat, there was only that quiet sense of something being missing… but above all else, there was happiness and there was hope. I stayed there for a moment, taking it all in – a once familiar sight almost alien to me now, and that's when Matthew slid a comforting arm around my shoulders.

I relaxed and stepped in.

*

A canopy of Autumn tree branches hung over my head as I stood by Granddad's memorial. The leaves from above lay in a jumble of crimsons and ambers at my feet; it had been my idea to plant a tree to commemorate him, and in his favourite season, it was the most fitting. A place I could truly feel connected with him.

'Hello, Granddad,' I began, as though it was him I was conversing with and not a plaque beneath a scrawny tree. 'You won't believe where I've been.'

I sat down in the leaves, crossed my booted feet and told him everything. I described the sun set in Perth, the magnificent foods in Bangladesh, the culture of China. I described Amala, and detailed my love for Matthew.

...And I told Granddad I missed him. I told him with tearful eyes and a tremble in my voice... and I held up the passport; not my 'future' copy, but my present. The one my grieving self needed so much.

A strangely confident part of me knew how to get the passport back – knew there was only one person up for the job.

I set it at the base of the tree trunk, kissed my fingers and pressed them there. Then I stood once more, ready to meet Matthew by the gates.

We departed hand in hand, the diamond ring on my left finger flashing in the Autumn light as we walked into our future.

*

It had been a whisper of a sound – something hitting something so softly it could have been placed down with human hands. Bemused, I looked around, and almost immediately my gaze settled on my bedside table... and the passport resting lazily atop it.

The Literary Vision

Henry saw her every day; same time, same place, same platform... Two dozen or so other commuters caught the train alongside him every weekday, battling the capricious British weather and erratic ticket office opening times of the tiny suburban station, to journey into the city for that looming 9am start – and *she* was always one of them, catching his eye without fail.

It wasn't that she was supermodel beautiful; Henry wasn't that clichéd. Nor had she ever seemed to notice him in return, drawing his glance through mutual agreement. It sounded silly when he said it out loud – which he only ever did over Saturday night pints down the local with his brother – but what really caught his eye about her wasn't the bobbed brown hair, feathered with layers, or the dark blue peacoat over her office skirts; it wasn't even the skirts themselves, although Henry couldn't help but notice them in passing, naturally.

No, what captured his attention most were the books.

Because – every day – without fail, she was sat on the platform, reading a book.

Yes, it sounded ridiculous, Henry knew that; Ben, his brother, had told him often enough. But she was *always* reading a book and in these days of Kindles and iPads and smart phones, yes, Henry found that eye-catching. And the speed with which the book changed too! She read fast, that much was obvious – he enjoyed turning up for the boring commute and trying to subtly catch a glimpse of the colourful paperback she was deeply engrossed in that day. The paper rustled in the breeze, the cover and spine always well-creased beneath her eager fingers and Henry simply found the whole sight entrancing at 8am: a small speck of rainbow imagination dotted amongst the sea of office blacks, browns, greys that filled the rest of the platform between them.

The first month she had started catching the train, Henry had noticed no less than five different books pass through her hands; the second month he had been watching with a little more of a passing interest and the count had shot up to seven: *Mostly Harmless*, *The Lady Vanishes*, *My Sister's Keeper*...

And then, three weeks ago, he had noticed her in the crowd of nameless, faceless passengers wearily journeying home on his 5pm route – it was the fiery orange of the paperback that had caught his attention; a pair of gates lit up by deep red and gold that faded into the rest of the black cover: *Rebecca*. He was sure he had seen it that morning... And then he had looked higher up to find her face above the cover, reading as intently as she had at 8am. From then on, it had become routine to find her on both journeys, almost always in the same carriage as him... After a week of this, Henry – spurred on by Ben's drunken urging – had determined to do something to catch her attention in return.

He contemplated reading a book too, perhaps prompting conversation, but quickly dismissed this idea. He was never awake enough in the mornings to focus his attention on anything more than watching the scenery roll calmingly past the window as they rattled through the countryside towards the urban sprawl of Manchester. Besides, if he sat down reading the same book as her when it wasn't something as culturally explosive as *The Da Vinci Code*, for example, how stalker-like would it look? Henry had already spent hours at the pub desperately musing with Ben over whether he was practically a stalker anyway; for God's sake, he knew the titles of her latest literary forages going back a month!

But he was twenty-eight years old and his last serious relationship had been almost two years ago; he last kissed a woman nine months ago, hadn't been on a date for six... Because, outside of University it was virtually *impossible* to meet anyone without looking like a stalker; you couldn't date colleagues without risking the unprofessionalism of post-break-up office sniping and, after about the age of twenty-four, pulling girls in loud, sticky clubs and bars lost something of its suavity. As Ben often liked to point out, this wasn't the 1950's anymore – you couldn't attend a dinner dance or a street party, meet the woman of your dreams and just whisk her off under the starlight. Now it was either the lucky dip lies of online dating, or the mortification of being set up with one of the other tragically single acquaintances of your "long-term couple" friends.

Since neither of those seemed like viable options until the bitter tang of desperation finally soured everything, Henry guessed he was left with this: trying to strike up a polite, witty, friendly conversation with the girl on the train. At least he saw her every day, so it wouldn't be too... weird.

So – again with Ben's drunken urging – Henry had determined that the next time he caught her eye, he would smile at her.

And to his surprise, it worked.

It was the 5pm journey home; Thursday, raining, with the dull grey of evening leeching away all enthusiasm as everyone realised that there was still another day left to get through before the weekend. They had boarded the train in the usual crush of barely restrained rudeness, everyone hurrying to grab their own seat at the cost of politeness; noticing a young, pregnant woman trying to move towards the aisles, Henry hung back and gestured for her to precede him, determined not to lose his own soul over the price of standing for the forty minute journey home.

With a grateful smile, the woman moved past him to the only remaining seat – right next to his literary vision. As the pregnant lady sat down, the reader glanced up from her novel and, noticing the woman's appreciative look, followed her gaze... straight to Henry.

He paused for a split second, heart thudding in his ears loud enough to drown out the music from his iPod – and then his natural delight at finding his plan so easily fulfilled overwhelmed his shock. An easy smile spread across his face, as he held her eyes – deep, hazel brown – thrilled to find himself locked into a moment with her finally.

The elation grew as, after a moment's surprise, she returned the smile, a slight blush creeping across her cheeks. Pressing her lips together, as if trying to shrink from the attention shared between them, she turned her eyes away and back down to her book. Henry watched her for a split-second more and then relinquished the moment, albeit happily.

She had smiled back – actually *smiled* back.

The way was paved, the scene was set...

Friday morning swapped another shy smile; the journey home, a brief nod accompanied it... A second week passed in the same vein, morning to night. The following Saturday, Ben slammed his pint down and demanded to know why Henry hadn't wrangled a coffee date yet – they both worked in the same city, for God's sake! But she always looked so absorbed by her book and Henry didn't want to come on too strong... He had swallowed his beer without tasting it; what was that about him not being so clichéd? Even so, they caught the same train every day, that was all – it made a nice quirk in their daily life, swapping a familiar smile and nod like veteran commuters... Could he really try to add another layer to that foundation, actually ask her out?

What if she said no?

His early morning spark would be snuffed out, the one interesting glimmer in his day tarnished by the feeling of rejection. Every paperback he glimpsed would be a reminder of what he had lost...

But, equally, could he live with not saying anything at all? What if he kept quiet, held onto the nods and the smiles like tiny treasures tucked inside a keepsake box – and then one day she just wasn't there anymore? He'd be kicking himself forever...

Perhaps he was over-thinking this.

Perhaps he should just seize the day, like Ben kept demanding belligerently.

As it turned out, Henry needn't have worried – because, come Tuesday evening, the day seized him.

*

Henry was late leaving work and, consequently, had to suffer the awkwardly panicked half-run, half-lumber that was the embarrassing symptom of dashing down the platform right on the last minute, fully visible to everyone both on his train *and* on the one waiting to depart opposite. He jumped the gap with roughly forty seconds to spare; one swift glance told him that there were no available seats, but for once there wasn't also a multitude of people crowding the aisles either. Henry briefly debated heading into the next carriage, or even the one further along from that, on the off-chance of finding an unoccupied place, but he always got on the first carriage – creature of habit. Plus moving along, banging open the connecting doors and muttering a constant stream of '*excuse me*'s would cause a stir – Henry's innate British nature cringed at the thought of drawing such attention to himself.

Besides, he suddenly realised, his literary vision was just across from him, seated by the window in one of the centre rows of three. She caught his eye as he straightened up, back resting against one of the glass partitions between carriages; the brief, familiar smile quickly followed and Henry decided that standing wasn't so bad really...

When she was once again immersed in her novel, Henry – under the pretence of eyeing the disappearing Manchester skyline out of the window – tried to sneak a glance at today's cover. To his surprise, the author's name was familiar to him, even if the title wasn't: Stephen King. The cover was orange, with a black mobile phone picked out in a Dali-esque style and black letters almost oozing the title across the front: *Cell*.

Henry blinked his gaze back up to the gentle face above the pages; the brown eyes, the thin reading glasses she quirked back up her nose every few minutes, framed by stray wisps of hair... He would never have pegged her as a horror fan – but then again, she did seem to read anything and everything...

With a sudden jolt, Henry realised he wasn't the only one in the carriage watching her intently.

The young man sitting opposite her, scruffy in a faded Oasis-fan kind of way, was firmly fixated on eyeing her up. Complete with natty, zipped-up parka and stubble that looked ten steps away from 'cool' and headed more towards 'degenerate', he couldn't seem to keep himself contained within his seat – every few seconds, his legs would twitch, his feet would tap, he would drum his fingers against his thigh and just generally shift irritably. With a sinking feeling, Henry realised that he could smell the alcohol wafting off the guy from his standing position, three rows back. No wonder the woman sat next to him was leaning unnaturally away from him and the window, the seat between them pointedly laden with her shopping bags. The two men completing book girl's row had their newspapers raised before their noses like shields.

The guy's eyes jumped from the novel in book girl's hands to the curve of her legs beneath her patterned skirt and back again. He was going to do something, Henry could tell. His stomach sank further.

'Good book, yeah?' The guy finally burst out; his voice was too loud within the tired, reserved stillness of the carriage. A few people looked over, everyone pretending not to hear whilst at the same time fascinated by this departure from traditional commuter rules. For her part, book girl pretended not to hear, clearly uneasy from the overpowering stench of alcohol wafting across to her. The guy's tone rose another notch. 'I said, good book, yeah?'

How could anyone be drunk at this time of day?

It was barely gone five-thirty.

Henry kept his eyes fixed on the situation; everyone in the carriage was pretending to do otherwise. Unable to avoid answering the man's question any longer, book girl lowered her novel slightly, looking over as fleetingly as possible.

'Erm, yeah, it's very good.'

'*Sca-aa-ry*, yeah?' He waggled his fingers, inebriated and Henry – along with the rest of his fellow passengers – watched uncomfortably as a creeping flush of embarrassment stole over his book girl's cheeks. Henry felt the same sense of cringing mortification as she obviously did; not necessarily for *her*, but for the palpable desperation of the drunk guy's advances. He wondered if he should look away, but he couldn't take his eyes from the scene – he felt protective of his literary compatriot and wondered if he should intervene...

'Yeah,' Book girl cast another fleeting look in the drunk guy's direction, fingers clutching the cover slightly tighter. Sadly, it didn't register.

'So what's it about?' He leant further forwards and book girl winced; hesitating a second too long, her silence became obvious – and the guy took offence. 'I said, what's it *about*?'

She opened her mouth, but it was too late – without warning, he snatched the book out of her hands and blearily started yelling out segments of the blurb on the back, clearly attempting sarcasm but not quite hitting the mark.

'The *Pulse* takes over... the *entire world*! Those re-rece-receiving *calls* would be infected...' He snorted derisively, gesturing dangerously at book girl, who recoiled, but still stoically held out her hand for her book. 'So everyone becomes *zombies* or something then?'

'Erm, yeah – can I have my book back please?'

'Hey, hey, come on, maybe I want to read it?' He jerked it out of her reach and the woman at the other end of the bank of seats tutted loudly; this only seemed to spur the drunk's aggression. 'Or what, am I not smart enough for stupid horror shit or something?'

'Look, please can I just have my book back?' She made another grab at it and, once again, the guy swung it out of her reach. He lurched to his feet and staggered into the aisle, still waving the book tauntingly in her face; Henry felt a surge of irritation for the way everyone else was just attempting to pretend this wasn't happening.

'If you want to be *scared*, baby, you don't need *books*...'

Henry felt a surge of fury; slinging his bag over one shoulder, he prepared to stride forward – but book girl had already leapt up and, with a surprising amount of courage, shoved the guy sharply backwards, snatching the fugitive novel out of his grasp. He staggered back in astonishment.

'You know what, you're not impressing anyone,' She snapped forcefully. The drunk swayed precariously in line with the train's rattle, eyes narrowing. Henry hovered anxiously on the edge of the scene, but book girl continued, gesturing angrily with her novel. 'Why don't you just sod off and bother someone else? Or better yet, sober up.'

The furiously waving book drove the drunk guy back another unsteady step; Henry was now just slightly between him and his literary vision, and he watched with a sudden mounting resolve to step in as the guy clenched his fists, spitting words back at her like gritty pebbles.

'Screw you, you little bitch – '

'Okay, mate,' Henry slipped in front of book girl, barring the drunk's way with both hands raised in a placatory gesture. 'I don't want to get involved here, but maybe you should just leave her alone, yeah?'

He risked a sidelong look at his literary vision, and paused as he found her dark eyes fixed on him; his heart rocketed with a second boost of confidence. The young drunk's eyes were also trying blearily to focus on him, but he was rocking ever more hazardously with every curve of the track – an ugly incident was on the brink of development here...

'Oh yeah? *Yeah?* Well, you know what, *mate* –' The guy swung out a fist and Henry jerked back, knuckles landing on open air barely an half an inch from his nose. A second shaky punch followed – Henry was vaguely aware of book girl shrieking something as he swung back out of the way again, striding back into the carriage entryway. The drunk guy lurched towards him in pursuit, and a second passenger rose to his feet too, aiming to join Henry in his attempted chivalry – but before he could get any further, the train shifted particularly sharply around a bend and the drunk found himself thrown forwards with the momentum, crashing against the opposite glass partition as Henry sidestepped quickly.

There was a moment of taut silence within the carriage, during which Henry was very aware of book girl standing close behind his shoulder, one hand clapped to her mouth. Stunned, their assailant looked up at them, unfocused and seemingly confused as to how he had ended up on the floor. Henry glanced around at the judgemental looks of their fellow passengers and ran his hand over the back of his hair; feeling slightly sorry for the guy, he extended a hand.

'Here, come on...'

The drunk reeled to his feet, fury spiking across his face. Ignoring Henry's outstretched hand, he batted the offer away with a clenched fist and stepped directly into Henry's path, glaring all the while. Raising an eyebrow, Henry squared his own shoulders, drawing himself up to his full height – and at six foot, he was well aware that he could look reasonably intimidating when he wanted to, although the courage he was clinging to was something that he had only ever had to muster once before, in a particularly tense bar brawl at Uni.

With the addition of the second passenger though, and the condescending looks of pretty much the entire carriage alongside them, it seemed to work – after glaring for another long minute, the guy staggered away, shaking his head and yelling, 'Screw you all anyway!'

Henry sighed as he watched the drunk's retreating back disappear down the carriage; the rhythmic clack of the train seemed suddenly loud in his ears – or maybe that was his heartbeat, because his literary vision was suddenly standing right in front of him, one hand resting on his forearm lightly.

'Hey, um – thanks. He was kind of starting to freak me out.'

'Yeah, well – no problem,' Henry smiled, a larger version of the last fortnight's exchanges. The easiest way to strike up conversation with his literary vision? Get into a fight with a drunk guy during the early evening commute – he should have thought of it sooner... Now that she was in front of him, she suddenly seemed even prettier too; her smile was slightly crooked, adding to the charm of her face, and there was a small smatter of freckles across her nose.

Henry realised he was staring and hurriedly cleared his throat. Casting his eyes down to the floor, he noticed the controversial item that had started all of this in the first place: her book, obviously knocked to the ground during the melee. Bending down, he quickly fetched it up, shifting the rescued novel from one hand to the other. 'Well – here you go. Sorry about... everything.'

'No, it – it was really... Thanks.' She took the book from him and held onto it for a second, before finally raising her eyes. 'You know, you just stood up for me and I don't actually know your name?'

'Huh? Oh,' Henry exhaled a laugh, sharing her awkwardness. 'Henry, I'm... Henry.'

'Henry – thank you. I'm Molly.' *Molly* – Henry had dreamt of discovering her name and now finally he knew. He would never have guessed it in a million years but... it suited her. She hung back a little now, glancing around the carriage; the passengers had gone back to their usual facade of pretending not to listen in, when actually they were hooked on every single sentence that passed between the literary damsel and her unexpected hero. Henry felt a burning urge to alleviate some of the blush that was returning to her cheeks.

'Well, I hope it's a good book – I'm not sure I could have gone to so much effort if he'd been trying to steal *Fifty Shades of Grey* off you,' he joked – then blanched.

What?

Was that even funny?

Thankfully, Molly seemed to find it so, as she grinned.

'If it had been *Fifty Shades of Grey*, I think I'd have let him have it.' She tapped the cover of the paperback with a fingernail. 'No, Stephen King is definitely worth it – he's an amazing writer; scary, but gripping.'

'Really? I've never read anything by him before... I've seen *The Shining* though – it was good...' Molly nodded, her entire expression lighting up.

'The book's better, believe me. You should try this sometime.' She held up *Cell* and Henry found himself nodding now, infected by her enthusiasm.

'Definitely – maybe I'll even get a copy tomorrow, given the rave reviews I'm hearing.' Molly narrowed her eyes slightly, as if sussing out whether he was teasing her or being genuinely serious. Another split-second of hesitation followed and then her smile suddenly turned coy.

'Or you could take this one? I've actually read it before – I guarantee you its good.' Henry opened his mouth, but she shook her head, that crooked smile widening. 'Seriously, I think you should read it – after all, you went to so much trouble to rescue it for me. Consider it a thank you.'

'Okay...' Henry found himself grinning too. Outside the window, the hazy sunset was just dipping over the horizon into dusk as the train sped on towards home, but to Henry it felt like the sun was shining all over his world. 'Sounds good – and I'll be sure to tell you what I think of it?'

'I'd like that,' Molly agreed, the flush staining her high cheekbones once more. She started to hand the novel over, but then paused, eyes narrowing again. Then, pushing her glasses up onto the top of her head to tangle into her dark hair, she suddenly began rooting around in her handbag. 'In fact... just so you don't forget...'

Triumphantly, she bore a biro aloft; opening the book to the inside cover, she clicked the nib out and scribbled something across the top of the front page. Finally done, she flipped the cover shut and held out the book to him, meeting his gaze warmly. Puzzled, Henry took the novel and glanced at the page: scrawled there in elegantly looped writing was her name, *Molly* – and a phone number.

Swallowing back a grin Cheshire cat wide, Henry raised the novel's spine to her and gestured vaguely with it.

'Believe me, I wouldn't forget.'

The train suddenly began to slow, several passengers around them clambering to their feet and reclaiming possessions, adjusting bags and coats... Henry glanced quickly out of a nearby window to find that they were nearing the first of the larger connecting stations on their route – there would be another two small stops, then his own – and Molly's – station, another bustling stop where more passengers switched trains, speeding off into the gathering darkness to wherever home was for them.

He stepped back out of the way as the train finally juddered to a halt; hissing for a moment in the cold evening air, the doors slid open and people began to stream their way out into the evening. To Henry's surprise, although she had moved back with him slightly, Molly turned the collar up on her coat and shifted her bag, angling half-towards the doors too. She smiled as Henry frowned.

'Different route tonight, then?' He asked the question before he could stop himself, flinching as a little voice inside his head flagged up *'Stalker!'* loudly. But, as with his clumsy joke before, Molly didn't seem to notice; instead, she stepped back a little further towards the door and the edge of the queue of people disembarking, still smiling back at him.

'Adventurous, right?' Hopping off the train to the platform edge, she paused for one last moment, glancing back. Further along, a whistle sounded. Molly nodded at the book still clutched in Henry's hands. 'Remember: tell me what you think... And thanks again – Henry.'

The doors started to slide shut, but Molly stayed where she was, holding the farewell between them. Henry darted forward, seizing the last second and raising the novel readily.

'No problem – Molly. And I will!'

The train started to move and, after another lengthy moment, so did Molly, ducking her head to hide her jubilant expression and sparkling eyes as she made her way towards the station exit, joining the throng. Henry remained where he was until she was completely out of sight, swallowed up by the charcoal-smudged outlines of bushes and hedgerows as the train curved around a bend and on towards its next destination. Exhaling a long breath, Henry turned to claim a seat – the carriage had half-emptied now, everyone heading for bigger and brighter towns only accessible from the illuminated pit-stop of that last connecting station.

He found himself met by the scrutinising gaze of those passengers remaining and now it was his turn to blush: they had all just witnessed his moment of chivalry, as well as his following efforts to chat Molly up... As he swung himself into one of the pairs of seats at the back, he suddenly shrugged the embarrassment off – after all, she had given him her number. *Him.* Who else there could boast such good fortune?

Henry sat for a couple of minutes looking out the window at the darkened skyline, reflecting on everything that had just taken place; he could hardly believe that the one thing he had been dreaming of for the past three weeks – three *months* even – had actually just happened. He kept sneaking surreptitious glances down at the book on his lap, convincing his mind that Molly, the drunk, his outrageous good fortune hadn't just been some warped hallucination. Henry would never have believed he could feel such a rush of appreciation for Stephen King before...

Perhaps he should start reading it now? He flipped open the cover, fully intending to satisfy his promise to Molly – plus what was it the drunk had said about zombies? Didn't sound too bad...

Try as he might though, Henry just couldn't focus – his attention kept springing back every few seconds to the front page and Molly's scrawled phone number at the top. Every number sent a quick thrill through his spine, heart leaping euphorically at the triumph. He would have to call Ben the second he got home – never mind the clap on the back from his brother, what he needed now was advice, because how soon was too soon? Molly had given him her number; she clearly wanted him to ring her... So should he call her tonight? Tomorrow morning? Perhaps he should text? Maybe he should text now?

No.

No, this was ridiculous – he was getting carried away. Firmly closing the book, Henry tucked it beside his leg, resting it against the lip of carriage wall beneath the window sill – out of sight, but still with its reassuring touch lightly reminding him how, suddenly, everything had changed. Drawing in a deep breath, Henry drifted back to looking out of the window, musing on his thoughts; yes, he'd wait until he got in, give Ben a ring and see what advice his suave younger brother had in store for him...

The next two stations passed without Henry really noticing properly. He was dimly aware of the overhead announcements counting down the stops until home, along with the carriage persistently emptying – it would only fill up again at his stop though, Henry knew. He had to love the erratic essence of train journeys; anything could happen, as he himself had just demonstrated... The buzz was slowly quieting into a steady bubble of elation, his adrenaline rush soothed by the steady rhythm of the train and the warm glow of his carriage reflected out into the gathering night. He had never felt so content.

As the tinny announcement sounded his stop through a fumble of static, Henry turned to gather up his shoulder bag and noticed an elderly gentleman struggling to lift his suitcase from the overhead rack, a cane flailing in the other hand. Fate really seemed intent on making Henry a knight in shining armour that evening; getting up quickly, he stepped forward and reached up, offering the man a polite, 'let me give you a hand with that'. The old man looked up at him, chest heaving from the effort, grateful for Henry's intervention.

'I used to be able to manage things like this,' He said apologetically and Henry shook his head, easing the suitcase to the floor.

'It's no trouble – I'm getting off here anyway, so let me get it onto the platform for you...' The old man seemed agreeable and Henry quickly hefted the bag towards the doorway; now that it was on the ground, where gravity could reassert itself, it seemed heavier than before – what did the old guy have in there, gold bars or something? Perhaps

Henry was just exhausted from so much chivalry in one day...

The evening chill hit him the second he stepped down to the platform, not entirely unwelcome, but cold enough to hurry Henry's step. He quickly set the suitcase down a safe distance from the platform edge and found the button to eject the pull-handle. Turning, he gestured to the old man and nodded in a finalised, '*good evening*' sort of way.

'Thank you, very kind,' The man nodded gruffly in response and Henry shrugged.

'Not at all.' With another quick nod, he turned away and began to head off down the platform, towards the exit, the main road, home... and Molly's book.

Wait.

Molly's book.

Henry stopped dead, the realisation hitting him like a bucket of icy water; his stomach flipped horribly and then seemingly attempted to crawl up his throat, churning nausea all the while. The book – the *phone number* –

Distracted by the struggles of the old man, he'd left the book *on the train*.

He spun around, but the guard was already blowing his whistle, preparing to hop back aboard and disappear off into the night; the last of the gaggle of passengers switching across from other trains had finished boarding already and the evening commute schedule was ticking on... Henry felt literally frozen with indecision for one hideously elastic moment – and then the monotonous warning beep that indicated the doors were about to close jerked him back into action: he *could not* lose that book.

Which left only one option.

Just as the doors began to slide shut, Henry sprinted the last two feet between him and the nearest pair – he was almost three carriages down from where he had gotten off, but that didn't matter right now – all that mattered was getting back on the train and retrieving that precious novel, regardless of how long it would take him to get home again afterwards.

'No! Wait!'

He threw himself between the doors; the gap was narrowed to almost Indiana Jones proportions, but he just managed to slip through, tripping over his own feet in the process and staggering with the momentum across the entryway to slam into the opposite side of the carriage. Pausing, Henry drew in a breath – and then felt the carriage shudder beneath his feet, the train moving off along the tracks once more. He'd made it – and the entire carriage, for the second time that evening, was watching him in surprise. At least he was making a fool out of himself in front of an entirely new set of people this time...

Henry straightened up, squaring his shoulders and briefly dusting off the front of his jacket, attempting valiantly to appear nonchalant. All that mattered now was getting Molly's book back; gathering his bearings, Henry set off hurriedly down the aisle towards the connecting door of the carriage.

Banging through the first set of doors, Henry hurried on towards the next – that was the section he had been sitting in, he was sure, even though the train was fuller now and his urgency was attracting more and more interested glances. That had definitely been his carriage; he remembered, from those first few minutes standing in the entryway, that it had been preceded by the compartment that held the bike rack... He wrenched open the last set of doors, crossing the precarious metal walkway that wobbled within the rubber-walls of the connecting passage. Just as he stepped across the threshold, into the carriage with the bike rack – so close to his final destination – he found himself brought to a sudden halt by the appearance of the ticket man, who straightened stiffly to bar Henry's path.

'Sorry, excuse me –' Henry began; the ticket man sniffed.

'Can I see your ticket please?'

'I – what?'

'Your *ticket*, please?' The man looked irritated at having to explain himself.

'Right, yes, erm...' Henry fumbled in his jacket pockets, desperately trying to remember where he kept his rail pass. As he patted himself down awkwardly, he craned his neck to surreptitiously try and peer past the conductor, attempting to locate his earlier seat – to his dismay he saw that two men had taken up residence in the spot, one glancing absently at a newspaper. So where was the book? He hastily switched his attention back to the ticket collector. 'Hey, erm –

has anyone handed in a book to you? Stephen King...?'

The conductor's eyes narrowed, obviously wondering whether Henry was trying to distract him from the issue of his ticket.

'A book? No, no one's handed in a book, sir. Now if I could just see your ticket, please?'

Henry felt flushed with desperation. He practically tore open his bag, fumbling around its chaotic innards for the tell-tale slick plastic cover of his railcard wallet; finally, he snagged it with a nail and hurriedly dragged it out, sighing with relief. The ticket man, on the other hand, was glaring at him in such a way that, if looks *could* kill, would definitely ensure Henry's place six feet under. He quickly thrust the pass at him.

'Are you *sure* no one's handed a book in? I left it behind you see – just now – I'm just trying to get it back... It was sort of a gift and –'

The conductor obviously wasn't listening; with another sneer, he stopped scrutinising Henry's pass and looked up at him.

'No one's handed me any books, *sir* – and I'm afraid this pass isn't valid.'

'*What*?' Henry's attention was only half on him – the men hadn't handed the book in, so that must mean that it was still on the seat, or at least somewhere around it... He distractedly glanced down at his pass, which the ticket officer was holding out to him pointedly. 'What do you mean, it isn't valid? It's a monthly pass – '

'Yes sir, it *is* a monthly pass, but for the line extending from Manchester to Macclesfield. We have just left Macclesfield and are now on route to Stoke on Trent. You'll need to purchase a separate ticket to cover that part of your journey...'

'No, no,' Henry shook his head emphatically, still trying to keep one eye on the men now in his seat – and quite possibly in possession of his book. 'That's what I'm trying to explain – I left my book here – well, it's not *my* book, it's someone else's and they gave it to me – I left it by accident just in the next carriage – I'm just looking for it –'

'Sir, if you are going to Stoke on Trent, you will need to buy a ticket –'

'I'm *not* going to Stoke on Trent, I just explained!' Henry's patience was wearing as thin as the ticket man's – if he could just reach those two guys and ask if they'd seen his book... The phone number jumped into his mind, unbidden, and his desperation rose a couple more notches. He took a couple of steps forward, gesturing down the carriage. 'Look, I'm just trying to find my book – I got on the train at Manchester, I got off at Macclesfield and realised I'd lost it – I just need to get it back, *please*...'

'Sir, if you don't buy a ticket, I will have to ask you to leave the train at the next station – with a fine!' As if backing up the conductor's words, and to Henry's consternation, the train began to slow: they were approaching Stoke on Trent already. Henry staggered as the train began to lurch into a more measured pace, lights springing up on all sides as buildings began to invade their surroundings.

To make matters worse, from over the ticket officer's shoulder, Henry saw the two men getting to their feet, gathering up their briefcases...

'Please – I just want...'

'Sir – '

The train rumbled to a halt and, as he watched the men head towards the doors, Henry knew that it was now or never – the thought of Molly, his literary vision, and her longed-for number potentially disappearing because of his own carelessness drove him to new, desperate heights.

He sidestepped the ticket officer and practically threw himself down the length of the aisle, incoherent yells chasing at his back. He was across the first entryway, pushing through the crowds waiting to disembark and halfway down the next aisle before he heard the bleeping of the doors as they slid open to spill passengers out onto the floodlit expanse of the concourse. The ticket officer was struggling against the tidal flow, torn between his duty to police new passengers and his bureaucratic need to chase Henry, the assumed ticket cheat... Daringly ignoring the man's cries, Henry kept on running.

It'll be there, it'll be there, it has to be there...

He reached the seat he had been sitting in, barely fifteen minutes ago –

It was empty.

Lunging over it, Henry batted at both chairs, then at the gap between them, as if by sheer force of will he could pluck the book out of thin air. He dropped to his knees and fumbled beneath the seat, both in front and behind: nothing.

The men – one of them must have taken it.

Henry leapt to his feet once more; weeks, no, *months*, pining after the possibility of ever getting Molly – née book girl – to look at him, let alone *speak* to him, and then she had handed him her number on a silver platter masquerading as a Stephen King novel?

He could not lose it – not now...

Hearing the warning beeps of the train at the last possible moment for the second time that night, Henry raced to the doors, once more turning into a very urban Indiana Jones as he threw himself through the closing gap one last time, shouldering bemused people out of the way as he did so. He scanned the crowds frantically – where the hell had those men gone? And then suddenly, further down the platform, he glimpsed one of them, heading for the stairs – but where was his friend? And was he the right one, the one with Henry's book and Molly's precious phone number?

By some miracle of chance, as Henry anxiously observed him, the man was knocked into by another traveller passing in a rush; caught slightly off balance, he was pushed into a half turn, one arm raising to steady himself in surprise – and clutched in his hand was the newspaper Henry had seen him reading on the train... It was curved around something else like a sling, something small and rectangular...

The book.

Henry ran pell-mell down the platform, yelling at the top of his voice, 'excuse me! *Excuse me!* Hey, wait!'

It felt as if the concourse had stretched out like a vast prairie, concrete endlessly rolling beneath Henry's feet as he tore towards the businessman from the train – six feet, two feet; when he was barely a couple of inches away the man suddenly seemed to realise that the shouts were directed at him and half-turned, shoulder moving into Henry's outstretched hand by accident, tugging him to a halt.

'Sorry, excuse me, I – I –' Henry sucked in a deep breath, trying to gather his wits. 'Sorry, but I – excuse me, I think that you have my – my book...'

The man stared at him, bewildered.

'I'm sorry?'

'On the train – I left my book? Well, it wasn't mine, it was given to me by someone else –' Henry realised that he kept repeating that, but no one would ever really understand the significance of Molly's interest except him, and perhaps Ben... He hurried on. 'Never mind – the thing is, I left my book on the train, right where you were sitting actually, and I think you may have picked it up?'

Henry gestured to the newspaper and the guy's perplexed expression ebbed slightly.

'Me? Sorry, but I'm afraid I can't help you – I don't really read books anymore, newspapers about all I can manage.' Now it was Henry's turn to look bewildered. The man flipped open his newspaper to reveal a small, black, leather-clad bundle contained securely within. Henry's heart sank, his breathing turning shallow. 'Since I got the Kindle, I find it easier on the commute.'

No.

No, no, no, no, no...

'Then your friend...?'

'Who, Barry? The guy I was sitting next to? We'd just had a business meeting, happened to be heading back the same way – I think he's got to go back to Birmingham tonight... Now you mention it, I think he did pick up a paperback as we were getting off back there – James Herbert... No, no – Stephen King, yeah, that was the one...'

Henry felt like his legs might actually give out from underneath him. The businessman seemed to notice his suffering because he pressed a sympathetic hand to his shoulder.

'Sorry, man – if he realised it belonged to someone, he'd be mortified.'

'He's going back to Birmingham?' Henry straightened up, clutching at the one hope he had left. The man nodded and Henry wasted no more time; pulling away from his benevolent grasp, he took off down the stairs, frantically seeking out a departure screen. Birmingham, Birmingham, Birmingham – it was his last chance... There, platform three – he had two minutes –

Henry ran like he'd never run before. The blood was pounding in his ears, the back of his throat tasted like iron filings and with every step Molly's number seemed to fade indistinctly before his eyes. Only the name of the Stephen King novel burned across his eyelids in ever-increasing irony:

Cell. The number that he was about to lose forever if he didn't make it in time...

His dream, his literary vision, it all rested on this moment...

The stairs to platform three blurred beneath his feet, the pounding of the asphalt matching the pounding of his pulse, and then suddenly the Virgin Pendolino was in front of him, steaming and hissing... And then there was that ever-ominous bleeping that was beginning to haunt Henry with its trilling, endless cry: the doors were starting to close.

He wasn't going to make it.

'No!' Henry yelled, sprinting furiously towards the nearest carriage. But the whistle had sounded even as Henry had been mounting the stairs and this time his Indiana Jones incarnation wasn't so blessed as before – third time lucky? As if.

The doors locked together and Henry pulled up short before he slammed against them cartoonishly. He screwed his eyes shut, unable to look, unable to bear the pain of how close he had been... The chugging, thundering squeal of the brakes being released shot through him like a knife and then the unmistakable sensation of the train pulling away knocked him back a few steps, albeit reluctantly.

It was over. He had lost the book.

Worse than that – he had lost Molly's number.

He was stranded in Stoke on Trent train station, having run two platforms and the entire length of a train in order to reclaim the most perfect looking book ever written because it had *her* phone number scribbled in the front of it. If it hadn't been for that god-damn ticket man, he might have actually stood a chance of not screwing up so spectacularly!

Because he had screwed up.

Henry could almost hear Ben's chiding tone ringing in his ears: *you see her every day, idiot – just ask her for her number again...*

But could he really do that? Really? Molly had given him that book in the spirit of good will, of mutual interest... He had just stood up for her when he didn't have to, when no one else looked like they were going to and, after weeks of smiles and nods, that was what it had taken to get them conversing. In all truth, Molly was a complete stranger to him – she had given him something of hers as a gesture, trusted him with it, this girl he had only just met – in fact, she had trusted him with something even more personal, her goddamn *phone number* –

And, within barely half an hour, he had lost it. How could he explain that to her without looking like an idiot? She'd think he wasn't interested in her, that he was making it up...

That he didn't care.

Slumping back against the wall, Henry pressed the base of his palms against his temples, wishing that if he could just concentrate hard enough he would simply be able to step back in time, to the moment Molly stepped off the train, leaving her book in his hands, so that he could replay those few seconds and *put the damned novel in his bag...*

Too little, too late.

Sighing heavily, Henry dropped his head to his chest, finally giving in.

The book was gone –

And so were his chances.

*

Wednesday morning came and Henry – after a long, hard talking-to from his brother – prepared for early-morning confession: he would just tell Molly the truth, come what may. He knew how absurd, how unbelievable it sounded... But he would just have to hope that, like his gawky jokes the night before, his literary vision would see the funny side.

But she wasn't there.

Belatedly, Henry remembered how she had gotten off a couple of stops earlier the night before; no wonder. Holding in a sigh, he turned away from her usual spot, its emptiness tarnishing that brief spark of optimism somewhat; confession would just have to wait until five thirty then...

But she wasn't there, either.

Thursday morning came and went: no Molly.

Thursday evening was a dull repeat; by the end of Friday – still no book girl – Henry had lost hope altogether. It was over – his worst fear had come to pass: she had changed routes. God, for all he really knew about her, Molly maybe had even moved house, relocating to a new area and a new commuting timetable – why shouldn't she? They were strangers, swapping smiles on the train into work; that situation was hardly long-term. That it had gone on for three months already without interruption for one of them was miracle enough!

And speaking of miracles, he'd had her phone number in his *grasp* – and he'd lost it.

She had probably wondered why he hadn't called; three days and nothing, not even a text. Henry had spent hours stoically attempting to recreate the mobile number on scraps of paper, but he could never get past the '077' without self-doubt and lingering fear kicking in to render the whole exercise completely useless. How could he have let the book out of his sight? He deserved to suffer for that stupidity.

Even Ben had no advice this time.

The weekend loomed and Henry could think only of the things he had let slip out of his grasp: what if this Saturday morning could have been spent with Molly in town, sipping coffee and discussing books? What if Saturday evening would have seen them head out to the cinema? He would never really know, not without the book and the beautiful scrawl of her phone number to guide him. All Henry was left with was his re-discovered DVD of *'The Shining'*, just the name of Stephen King making him feel like all ties with his mysterious, freckled, literary brunette weren't completely severed.

Perhaps, come Monday morning, she would be sitting on his platform once more, nose buried in a brand new paperback?

Henry hoped for that scenario more than anything – but he doubted his luck would hold... He had really screwed this up. He didn't even know her second name.

Just Molly.
Beautiful, elusive, literary...
Molly.

*

Monday morning came and Henry headed onto the platform at 8am, barely raising his eyes from the white Styrofoam lid of his cardboard take-out cup of coffee. What was the point? Three days in a row she hadn't been there, with her flowered skirts and blue peacoat, absently pushing her reading glasses up her nose as she devoured page after page... It was beginning to physically ache, the anticipation of seeing her only to find an empty space on the bench, disappointment souring the eagerness irreparably.

Stifling a sigh, Henry knocked back another swig of coffee – and froze mid-sip.

Out of the corner of his eye... No, it couldn't be... He was surely so desperate to see her petite frame that he was imagining things in his optimism... Surely?

No. No, this time, it was real.

She was *there*.

Henry almost choked on his coffee. As he spluttered, Molly looked up – and frowned.

'Henry?'

'Molly!' He hastily checked himself, realising how overwhelmingly animated he sounded. She rose from the bench, starting towards him and he hastily wiped smudges of spilt caffeine from his lips. 'Hey – I've been looking for you, all last week –'

'Yeah, I was staying with my sister – she's had the flu, needed someone to look after her for a couple of days...' Henry stared at her, resisting the urge to laugh hysterically at his own stupidity. Of course; of course, it would be something *so* simple – how could he have gotten so carried away? First he lost the book, then he decided he was never going to see her again because she hadn't happened to be on the train for a couple of days – and first and second place in the Idiot Prize go to...! Molly meanwhile was looking up at him shrewdly, eyebrows raised. 'So... you have something to tell me then?'

How did she know?

'Well, yes.' Henry paused, fumbling for words; now that the moment had come and his prayers had been answered, he had no idea what to actually say. His grip tightened on the coffee cup. 'Look, it's about the book...'

'Yeah, you never called –'

'It wasn't because I didn't want to, believe me –'

'I know,' She interrupted and Henry froze for a second time.

'You – you know?'

'Yeah. You lost my book.' Henry's mouth dropped open. How on earth...? Molly grinned at his evident surprise. 'It was kind of funny actually – at about nine o'clock on Wednesday morning, I got this phone call – for a minute I thought it was you, which I thought was cute, being so eager and everything... But it was from this guy in Birmingham, which was weird, because I don't know anyone in Birmingham. Turns out he found this book on a train? He thought someone had left it because they were done with it, but when he started reading it later that night, he found my name and phone number in the front and figured it must have been left behind by mistake...'

Henry was like a deer in the headlights; he could feel the humiliating fire of red spreading across his cheeks as she watched him, amused. Finally, after an age stretched between them, Henry managed to exhale an embarrassed laugh.

'Yeah – about that... Look, I got up to help someone and I just... I don't know what happened. The second I got off the train, I realised what I'd done and I practically killed myself getting back on to find it – in fact, a ticket officer is pretty sure I'm some sort of punk who likes to cheat the national rail system, and then I had to chase a guy down the platform at Stoke on Trent, then almost got on another train to Birmingham trying to get your book back...'

'I know,' Molly's smile widened, dark eyes soft. Henry was incredulous.

'You know that *too*?'

'The man who found *Cell*, who rang me up? He said he'd gotten a call just before he rang me, from a colleague in Manchester whom he'd had a meeting with the day before... *He* also thought maybe the book belonged to someone – because he'd been accosted by some desperate guy off the train, who was trying to find his book...'

Henry winced.

'Yeah, that'd be me...' Molly raised her eyebrows again and Henry sighed. 'Look, Molly, I'm so sorry – it was a complete accident and I feel like such an idiot – '

'No,' Molly caught hold of his arms, shaking her head earnestly. 'No, don't be daft – Henry, you ran the length of one train, apparently got stranded at Stoke on Trent and were prepared to go all the way to Birmingham, just to get my book back.'

'Well – honestly? It was your phone number I was more worried about.'

Molly laughed, the most amazing sound Henry had ever heard.

'You're crazy – and really, *really* sweet. You could have just asked me again.'

'I was worried you'd think... I don't know, that I didn't really care? I mean, I lost your book – and I really did want to read it. And call you, obviously. This is ridiculously embarrassing.'

'Well, I think you've proved that you care, even if it is the most insane thing I've ever heard. And you already helped to save me from a drunk guy.' She narrowed her eyes at him, lips curling; pushing her reading glasses onto her head in a tangle that was becoming strangely familiar to Henry, she fumbled into her handbag. 'And I think I can help you out about the book... You see, the guy very kindly posted it back to me...'

Henry stared in astonishment as she produced a now slightly-more-battered copy of *Cell* from her bag, offering it to him once again. Unable to stop himself, Henry started laughing, tapping the cover fondly; flipping open the inside cover, he found the phone number still perfectly intact at the top of the page.

'Unbelievable.'

Molly's fingers brushed over his.

'Guess you still have my number too.'

Henry held her gaze, more content in that single moment than he had ever been in his life. He didn't even care that half the platform was earwigging in, nor the cold that nipped and bit at their fingers as they quietly held the book between them – the source of so much trouble, and yet still so much happiness.

Ben was never going to believe this...

Seize the day, Henry.

'You know what – forget the number. Let's go for a drink, yeah?'

'Ah, the direct approach. In case you lose the book again, hm?'

'Believe me, I'm never letting it out of my sight.' Henry smiled, shaking his head. 'No, I'm asking *because* I lost the book. I thought I wasn't going to ever see you again, stupid as it sounds. That's what I'd like to make sure doesn't happen. Come on, you can tell me all about the other books you like that I can accidentally leave behind on trains. How about it – Molly?'

Their train rumbled up the platform, the clank and rumble like a familiar friend; around them, fellow commuters began to stir and shift their belongings, heading for the doors, but together the intrepid book-hunter and his beautiful, elusive book girl hung back, blushing into one another's eyes. Finally Molly nodded, biting her lip as she delivered the answer he'd been dreaming of.

'Sounds great – Henry.'

His literary vision beamed and the whole world lit up; together they turned towards the train. Finally, after days, weeks, months, they were finally walking beside one another into the carriage, sitting down next to each other, talking and laughing – together. A bubble of happiness radiated out of their sunny smiles to infect the entire carriage, the fugitive novel still held between the intrepid book-hunter and his beautiful literary vision like a talisman, while their train clattered in the background like thunderous applause echoing off into the promise of the early-morning sky.

Daffodils

She stands and watches him, and she says nothing. For a long time, he hasn't been able to bring himself to say anything either.

Today, clutching a bunch of baby's breath – her favourites, back when they were together – he swallows down the fear, and starts the conversation.

'Hi,' he begins, and his voice catches in his throat, whipped away by fear. He wishes they weren't standing how they are now – her, stony faced, wreathed in broken memories and emptiness – and him, accepting that it's over, and hoping that she'll understand. 'I need to tell you something.'

'We need to talk,' Luna said softly, sitting down beside him on the sofa. The TV was a dull murmur in the background, and blue flickered from the screen onto the opposing walls, darkened by the evening. John caught her eyes, and turned down the six o'clock news in order to give her his full attention. Her eyes crinkled at the corners, making a sad smile worse, and she took in a quivering breath. 'Things aren't good.'

'I'm…' His eyes close, and for a moment he forgets how to speak. The cold steals his voice, squirrels it away with dread, and guilt. All inflection ebbs, and when he speaks, he sounds nothing like himself at all. 'I'm seeing somebody else.'

She offers no reply – of course not – and he immediately holds out the flowers in a pathetic peace offering. Several petals fall and dance, cast away by the light spring breeze. Even the daffodils are struggling to show their faces – no yellow jazz hands to brighten the morning, he relents. Why should they?

'Oh, look at those,' Luna beamed, and John watched her with fond eyes; she was still so beautiful, even when the cracks had begun to show. He fixed the bunch of flowers into the vase on her bedside – dainty white blooms crowding bright yellow trumpets. They brought the room to life, and Luna, too- for the first time in months. John couldn't believe such a simple thing as roughly cut flowers could inspire such hope.

He regrets the way he sounds, like a radio station losing signal, and he shakes his head as he realises that he's being absurd. He wonders why he needs her to be okay with this, especially now; especially with things the way they are. He has an attachment to long ago, to love lost, and yet he feels guilty about love regained. Why should he cling to the corpse of a marriage, to two years of unsaid things?

'She's called Hannah,' he continues, and as he mentions her name, his voice regains colour, and for a moment, the daffodils don't seem so far away. 'I met her in the museum, about two months ago. We've been commenting on each other's books for a while.'

John had been holding back the tears for weeks. It was far worse in public - they hovered behind the squint in his eyes and the hard line of his lips. Perhaps that was why she had noticed him.

"The Osiris legend is fascinating, isn't it?" she said, and the light admiration in her voice made John look up. She laughed, all Cupid's bow lips and friendly blue eyes, and he smiled in return. She gestured to the cabinet of ancient figures to dispel confusion, and he nodded in embarrassment. "It's one of my favourites." She grinned.

The museum suddenly became more than lovely relics, and it would for a while afterwards.

You're leaving me behind? She glares, and he shakes his head, urgently trying to put his mind to rest.

'You left *me* behind!' He argues, and his eyebrows knit in frightened heartbreak, fist curling around the rough ends of the small bouquet he holds. 'I…' He shakes his head, knowing she wouldn't say that, not really, and she certainly wouldn't mean it. He simply fears.

Oh God, does he fear.

What would the neighbours think? What would the relatives think? They'd blame him, watch on from their judgmental pews and point, and question him with brash barks on the past two years, and indeed, the ten years of marriage, and they'd tell him to think of the kids… but isn't he allowed to be happy?

'I need you to be okay with this,' he reasons, biting his lip. 'She's not a replacement. She's not. But she's… warm, and she understands. She knows how to make me happy. God, Luna, do I need to be happy.'

Kids fed, cat out, alarm set for the groggy morning, John settled on the edge of the mattress, hands running over his drawn features. He still couldn't look at the empty space in the bed. It beckoned him with resentment, lost time and loneliness, but he couldn't bring himself to feel those things. He only knew he missed her.

There is silence. Biting silence, in which flowers grow, and branches rustle and creak. Distant cars whisper by, passing footsteps clack on paved pathways. He waits for something to give, but of course it doesn't. What does he expect? For her to throw her arms around him, tell him that it's alright? For the clouds to part, and the spring to arrive? He wishes it was all so easy. He wishes he isn't here at all.

Yet he is. The fact is that he has found somebody else. Love must make way for love, and despite the secrecy, the private meetings in coffee shops, and tender kisses on cab back seats… Here he is, telling his wife about the new woman in his life.

'Hannah told me to come and tell you. I was nervous, but…' He bends down, and he sets the flowers at his feet. 'I know you'd want me to be happy.'

She stopped at the door, one bag slung over her shoulder – stuffed with things she needed, but didn't want. He followed her, leaning against the door frame, watching her with sad eyes. He'd have stopped her if he could.

She noticed, and cupped his face - so gentle. Despite everything; her eyes still smiled even though she didn't look like herself anymore.

No words were exchanged, just mutual understanding.

He steps back, and nods towards the arch of the gravestone, charcoal grey with fine, gold script across its front. It displays her name beautifully, and his own, just beneath, proclaiming him as a loving husband, when he feels the opposite now he has somebody else.

Tufts of unopened daffodils edge the grave, splashing green on an otherwise pallid backdrop. It is normally one of the more modestly beautiful graves in the cemetery, but the late spring and haphazard baby's breath only make it look sadder.

'Forgive me,' he says, in a voice so soft the wind masquerades with it and carries it away.

He heaves a sigh, and gives his wife's grave one last smile, before kicking his heels and leaving, hands buried in his pockets, head bowed. Around him, the cemetery is still asleep; false flowers waiting in fresh dirt, raindrops beading on stone angels wings, row upon row of the painfully missed and sorely forgotten.

By the stone, beneath the date of death – two years ago now, yet so recent – the first daffodil blooms.

And one by one, slowly but confidently, so do the rest.

Remember, Remember

Remember, remember, the fifth of November...

Without meaning to, Sophie found her footsteps beating out the steady rhythm of the nursery rhyme as she rounded the last corner and headed up the muddy track to the village recreation ground – the "wreck", as she and the rest of the village kids called it, due to its scruffy, time-worn, but well-loved, appearance.

It was basically a field that had been glorified after the War as a place to kick a football around, or bat a cricket ball haphazardly during the summer. Then the village fetes and maydays had thrown in their lot, until finally one rare, hot summer in the late '70s saw the installation of a children's playground at one end, beneath the willow trees. A couple of picnic benches added a decade later marked a dividing line between the playground and the sports pitch that still formed the bulk of the grassy area.

And tonight, as per traditional holiday usage, the "wreck" was home to a shambling assortment of fairground rides, toffee-apple stands, fireworks and shrieking kids running wild everywhere...

Bonfire Night.

Sophie couldn't believe that it had come around again already. She paused by the gate, watching the scene that was silhouetted in shadows before her, flickering against the pitch black night sky. It was freezing cold; Sophie had been forced to assemble the full winter wardrobe against the biting wind, her hat, scarf and mittens firmly in place, although she couldn't stop her unruly straw-blonde curls from blowing across her face even with the woolly beanie. She was going to have to watch that later, lest it get tangled in the sugary goo of the toffee-apples and candy-floss that always accompanied the firework finale.

Always.

Sophie was beginning to grow dubious about that word. For the past sixteen years, she had never really known anything different than "always" for her and her best friends, Louise and Debbie. The three of them had been friends since reception class and every year saw them uphold the same traditions and jokes... Bonfire Night was no exception; they would *always* go to the wreck, they would *always* bypass the bigger carni rides for the spinning teacups and they would *always* eat enough sugar to make their legs twitch when they finally returned home and sat down for hot chocolate and a few eternal episodes of 'Friends'.

Only this year they had turned sixteen and, without warning, everything had changed – as if this milestone in teenage birthdays had exploded something at the back of Louise and Debbie's minds that had been threatening to detonate for a while. Their old interests had suddenly snapped into nothingness, melted by the flooding hormonal acid of fashion, boys and an endlessly trivial interest in the minutiae of celebrity lifestyles.

The sixteenth birthday meltdown didn't appear to affect everyone though, Sophie reflected bitterly; although she didn't exactly *hate* any of those things, her interest in them definitely didn't extend to the pedestal-heights Lou and Debs held them at... She'd rather read, or watch a movie with a mound of popcorn, or go out and play basketball at the wreck – things Lou and Debs told her were *boring, fattening,* or else *might break a nail...*

She was beginning to irk them, Sophie could tell.

But they were beginning to irk her just as much.

Steeling her nerve, she plunged on into the Bonfire Night fray, which was mainly made up of kids, although a few adults were clumped together in groups around the edges, mainly parents of the younger children. It was one of those rare village-run occasions where guys and girls of all ages could hang out together, regardless of the usual social boundaries and barriers, and so the night was a teeming mass of raucous screams, yells and laughter. The darkness of the sky above them, spattered with stars, and the flashing lights of the fairground rides merged people with their shadows, until the field gave the illusion of being twice as full.

Sophie looked around vaguely for her friends. The bonfire was a huge mass of burnt orange at the other end of the wreck, burning steadily like a beacon in the middle of the roughly marked football pitch; just behind it was a rustling line of safety tape, halting children who might unwittingly approach the regiments of unlit fireworks that were waiting for the crux of the evening. The figures warming themselves beside the fire's rosy glow were flickering, distorted shapes, moving spasmodically as they chatted and laughed. Sophie's stomach rumbled at the thought of a huge bag of sickly-sweet candy-floss, munched beside the bonfire's crackling roar – the cosiest scene she knew. Now just to find Lou and Debs and she could get started on making it a reality...

After a few seconds of scanning, Sophie finally caught sight of the two girls perched on the unnaturally stationary roundabout with a couple of other girls from the year – and a cluster of boys. Sighing, Sophie headed over.

'Soph!' Debbie waved enthusiastically as she approached, looking eerily and unnecessarily glam in the flickering light of the bonfire that raged off in the distance behind them. Sophie noticed, her stomach plummeting like a rock as she did so, that both girls were wearing garish pink wellies with chunky, "high" heels – the kind Sophie hated because, well, was there anything more pointless? Wellies were meant to be for muddy walks and splashing through puddles – they weren't *designed* to have ridiculous heels that would damage their practicality.

Then she noticed that all the other girls in the group – vague blurs of names and faces from school who, without the uniforms, just merged into one indistinguishable mass of bleached hair and orange foundation – were wearing the same boots as her friends.

Sophie suddenly felt horribly conspicuous in her plain green, flat wellies...

They didn't even have a pattern, horror of horrors.

'Where've you been, Soph? We've been waiting for an *age*.'

'Sorry, I got held up – Mum – '

'Yeah, we've been at least twenty minutes waiting for you,' Louise interrupted her, although her gaze remained upon Dan Stockett, who was scuffing his trainers against the softened asphalt of the playground and chatting with a couple of other boys. He thought he was David Beckham, the class "premier" footballer; unfortunately for him, nothing could be further from the truth. 'We were just about to go on the 'Spin Doctor'; it looks awesome this year.'

No, it pretty much looks the same as it does every other year, Lou.

Sophie bit her tongue, swallowing the retort quickly.

'So you coming?' Debs was already on her feet, the group lurching towards the whirling lights of the fairground rides, where other kids were already clumped in straggling lines. Sophie opened her mouth, but already Debs was listening to the chatter of another girl and Sophie felt a molten knot of irritation clasp her at stomach again.

'Actually, I'm starving so I might just skip this ride and go get something to eat.' That seemed to get through, since both Debs and Lou turned to look at her, bemused. They'd surely realise now, right? Hang fire for a few minutes, go with her for toffee apples and hang out, just the three of them again – right?

'Oh,' Louise pulled a face, half-surprised, half-dismissive. 'Well, if you're sure.'

Sophie felt the molten knot climb higher, burning her gullet.

'Come *on*, Sophie! It's the 'Spin Doctor'; you can eat after!' Debs at least was trying to keep her included – it was just too bad that Sophie knew how quickly that loyalty would waver as soon as they reached the ride. Half the summer holidays and two months stuck in school together had already proven to Sophie how much things had changed; their old gang of three had been sacrificed for the wider crowd... So why was she so surprised now?

'No, seriously, Debs – I'm starved. I'll just go and – '

'You're really not coming?' Sophie felt tongue-tied; she desperately wanted her oldest, closest friends to think highly of her - but equally she couldn't hide away how much she just ended up feeling like a stupid little kid around them these days. She was blushing furiously now – a beetroot beneath a grape-purple beanie – and she could feel Debs glaring daggers into the back of her neck. Lou, meanwhile, was gone; linked with Daniel Stockett, her laughter shot back to Sophie, too high, and the irritation boiling her blood finally overtook the flush of embarrassment. Her stupid, so-called friends only wanted to go on the stupid ride to "accidentally" fall against the clueless boys, screaming girlishly all the while –

She'd rather just have her toffee apple by the bonfire.

'Yeah, I'm fine – I'm actually really hungry, so... I'll just grab some food and wait for you guys by the railings or... whatever...'

Sophie trailed off as Debbie frowned at her, looking as though food was something so un-cool she'd actually never heard of it before. Then, with a dismissive shrug, she turned away to rejoin the others: no backwards glance.

Always; yeah, right.

Bristling, she turned her back just as deliberately on the superficially chattering group, squaring her shoulders in the direction of the bonfire and food – the night's only potential salvation. The warmth of the fire smouldered against her cheeks, the logs crackling and snapping above the voices and laughter of neighbours and friends. About fifteen feet from the bonfire, Sophie paused, deliberating the stands: toffee apples or candy-floss? She could even go for a hotdog, but it seemed less fitting somehow...

She was veering towards the pink, sickly-sweet fluff of some candy-floss (less embarrassing to try to eat in front of the others, lest they find her again after their ride) when she saw it – and her heart froze mid-beat.

'Hey!' The yell burst from her chest and Sophie took off running, ignoring the strange looks from surrounding teens; how the hell had no one else noticed him? 'Hey! Zach! *Zach!* What do you think you're *doing*?'

Sophie had curved around the side of the bonfire, nearing the hazard tape that was flapping in the November breeze; up this close, the flames were sizzling hot, the sparks miniature firework explosions above the smoking logs and debris. Lurking in the shadows, just beneath the hazard tape, was a small figure, crouched on his hands and knees, poking a long stick into the burning embers with the naivety of the very young towards his safety.

'Zach!' Sophie repeated, her voice tight with panicked, but subdued, volume. 'Get away from there now, what the hell do you think you're *doing*?'

The little boy – nine years old, her next-door neighbour and frequent babysitting charge – looked up with large brown eyes, bemused at her anger. Sixteen now and yet still really fun, Zach idolised Sophie and, although she complained that she was too old for the job now, secretly she liked him just as much. He was a sweet little kid, funny without realising it and deeply intelligent; he had an almost scary aptitude for constructing things and could solve a Rubik's cube in three minutes flat. Which was why Sophie was so surprised to find him playing somewhere so dangerous.

Taking hold of his arm, she managed to draw him a couple of feet away before he wriggled out of her grasp; crouching to her knees to level with him, she gave him her most serious and adult look.

'Zach, you need to come away from the bonfire *now*, it's not safe. What were you thinking?'

'But I can't leave yet – I have to make sure it's in properly!' The boy protested, turning his gaze back to the fire. He was a skinny thing, with a mop of deep brown hair that was almost-black; his ears stuck out a bit beneath his woolly hat, in that little-kid fashion that hovers on the cusp between childhood and adolescence. In the gleaming orange glow of the fire, Sophie could see the freckles smattering across his nose – just as cute as hers had been when she was nine. At sixteen, they just made her feel awkward, peppering her pale skin.

'Make sure what's in?'

Zach's answer almost toppled her to the ground in surprise.

'The phoenix egg.'

'Wh-what?'

'The phoenix egg,' Zach repeated, looking up at her as though she were stupid.

'Oh-kaaay,' Sophie paused, wondering what sort of strange game this was; a quick glance around, though, told her that Zach was as on his own tonight as he was every other day. His parents had just had another "miracle" baby, their time currently devoted to the six-month old in a way that Zach was finding it hard to compete with. He didn't usually resort to dangerous activities to get attention though... 'So, you were putting a phoenix egg in the bonfire to...?'

'That's how phoenixes are born, Sophie.' Zach's voice definitely had an undertone of *"jeez, don't you know anything?'* to it this time. 'They come out of the flames.'

'Well, yeah,' Sophie was at a bit of a loss. 'But I don't think they mean bonfires. Look, come away, yeah – it's really dangerous to be so close, Zach.'

'But I need to make sure it's in far enough, otherwise it won't hatch!'

With a sigh, Sophie leant forwards, peering through the swaying flames into the dark heart of the bonfire's burning, criss-crossed wooden base. The heat made everything blur hazily, like petrol fumes over tarmac in the heat of summer. She shook her head.

'Well, I can't see anything, Zach, so I think it's pretty far in, okay?' Gently seizing his elbow once more, she tugged him back from the fire and the hazard tape; this time he went with her, albeit reluctantly.

'Do you really think it'll be okay?' He looked up at her anxiously and Sophie paused in her sweep of their immediate surroundings – thankfully no one else seemed to have noticed Zach in his efforts to become a real-life Guy Fawkes.

'Yeah, Zach – I think it'll be fine.'

The nine year-old looked back at the bonfire once, uncertain. Sophie rolled her eyes and tousled his hair, a familiar gesture that only she could get away with.

'So where did you get a phoenix egg then? You don't really come across them outside of Harry Potter World.'

Zach shot her another surprised look and Sophie swallowed back a grin; Zach had a fantastic ability to seem both incredibly wise and incredibly innocent at exactly the same time, with his wide-eyed, gap-toothed, matter of fact smile and huge eyes.

'In the supermarket.'

'Huh - in the supermarket. Really?'

'Yeah. Mum sent me to get some eggs and it was there in the egg box when we got home. It must have gotten in there by mistake.'

'Must have,' Sophie agreed, leading him back towards the sweet stalls with a hand on his shoulder. 'Aren't phoenix eggs pretty huge sorts of eggs though? I'm sure I read that somewhere.'

'Well, it was a box of *large* eggs.'

At that Sophie had to laugh.

'Okay, well I guess that explains it, yeah. So did you show your Mum?'

Zach pulled a face, lowering his chin so that his expression was lost in the night's deep shadows and covered by the orange glow of the fire behind them.

'She's always too busy with Rosy.'

Sophie felt a sharp shard of sympathy cut through her and she stopped humouring him, instead halting mid-step to crouch down beside him again and crook the corner of her mouth in an understanding, earnest smile.

'Yeah, I know it must feel like that a lot, Zach. But you know, Rosy's going to get bigger pretty quickly and then she won't need your Mum and Dad to look out for her – she's going to want her big brother instead. And that's pretty cool.' She nudged his shoulder. 'And I bet your Mum wishes she could spend time playing with you too – babies aren't anywhere near as fun as finding phoenix eggs at the supermarket, trust me. And she can't come to Bonfire Night with little Rosy, can she? Which sort of sucks for your Mum.'

Zach considered this intently, biting his bottom lip.

'Is your Dad here?'

'Luke's mum brought us – me and Luke and Harry. But after she gave us some money for the tea-cups, she went off with some of the other mums and told us to come and find her when we wanted to go home.' *Wow, responsible*, Sophie thought, rolling her eyes to the skies, where the stars twinkled their own disapproval. 'I wanted to help the phoenix so I told Luke and Harry that I was going home early and to say Dad came to get me.'

'That's actually quite ingenious, Zach – nice.' Sophie knew she probably shouldn't be encouraging lies, but for a nine year-old that was a pretty foolproof way to slip off unnoticed. She certainly would never have come up with such a plan at his age. Zach's parents still trusted Sophie to be a mature example to their son, though, so...

'You know that it was still a really dangerous thing to do though, yeah? Playing with fire, sticking things into the middle of the bonfire – you could have been really hurt, Zach, not to mention if anyone else had seen you, you'd be in so much trouble. You must *never* do anything like that again, okay? I'm serious here, Zach, okay?'

Zach nodded guiltily. He knew how risky it was; Sophie could see it written all over his earnest little face and decided to end her lecture there. He was a bright kid, and it was probably more effective for him to be told off by *her* than by anyone else. And all because of an egg; she knew Zach was imaginative, but jeez. Rosy must be sucking up more of his parents' attention than Sophie had originally thought.

'Come on then – let's go get some candy-floss and wait for the fireworks, yeah?' His face brightened as though the sun had just come up. As they headed over to the stand, Sophie couldn't help but ask him one last question, curiosity getting the better of her. 'Zach, why did you decide that the egg needed to go in the bonfire? Couldn't you just have hatched it in the oven or something?'

'Phoenix eggs don't hatch in the oven, Soph.'

'Right.'

'They hatch in proper flames – big orange and red ones, like in all the picture books. And then when the phoenix gets old and dies, it burns up again and another one comes to hatch out and take its place – so it never really dies at all, it just turns into something new and better and really, really cool.'

'Right,' Sophie repeated.

'My book of myths and legends says that phoenixes look like flames too – all their feathers are orange and yellow and gold, and when they fly they leave a trail of shooting stars and sparks and stuff? The egg needed to hatch, so I *had* to help it. I just couldn't think of a fire big enough. And then I remembered about tonight and the bonfire – I think it should work, Sophie. You know, it's going to be so cool when it hatches...' He paused, looking concernedly in the direction of the bonfire once more. 'As long as I got it in far enough... They need loads of heat, you know?'

Sophie handed him a bag of candy-floss, smiling as she untwisted the knot of her own.

'I think it'll be fine, Zach. Honestly.'

They were just turning from the stand when darkened figures approached from the left, giggling and jostling each other. Louise and Debbie. Sophie's heart sank.

'Soph! Oh my god, you should so have come on the 'Spin Doctor' with us – it was *amazing*! The guys are waiting for us – we're going on again; you should really come this time.'

Zach raised his dark eyes to her, candy-floss reddening his lips in a sugary hue and Sophie's heart plummeted even further. This was so not cool.

'We-ell – aren't the fireworks about to start?'

They always stood gazing at the fireworks together, enraptured by the display...

Always.

'Oh, *come on*, Sophie – fireworks, seriously?'

'Yeah,' Debbie agreed, 'the fireworks are always the same every year – the rides are way more fun! And anyway, you'll still be able to see the sky, won't you?'

'I don't really think it's the same, Debs.' Sophie deadpanned, unable to help it.

'Sophie, fireworks are for the *little kids*.' Louise sniffed, shooting a dismissive look in Zach's direction. 'We came all the way over here to find you while the others went on the Twister; I can't believe you're being so... un-cool.'

Finally: the word was out in the open.

Sophie shrugged her shoulders, feigning nonchalance even as her blood boiled.

'Sorry to be so *disappointing*, Lou, but I just bought candy-floss and Zach and I were planning to watch the fireworks. So... I guess I'll just catch up with you guys later.'

Louise harrumphed, while Debbie just stared at her in complete amazement, as though Sophie had just sprouted four more arms.

'You're seriously going to hang with him? He's a *kid*.'

'So? Since when were you two too cool for fireworks and playing games?'

'You're being so lame, Sophie.' Was all Louise could manage in retort. Ever the peacemaker, Debbie eyed her one last time, gesturing back towards the garish glow of the carni rides.

'Come on, Sophie, seriously. We just want to have a laugh and it's not like he's *your* responsibility. Do you seriously want to spend all night babysitting and not even getting paid for it?'

'You know what?' Zach's face had crumpled at their words and suddenly Sophie stared at her friends as though seeing them for the first time; they weren't the same Lou and Debs from reception class, from their first day at high school, even from last summer. She didn't like it – and she didn't want to be a part of it anymore either, even if it meant teen-clique suicide. 'Why don't you two just *grow up*.'

Something splintered in that moment; strangely Sophie didn't care. For a long moment, Louise and Debbie stared her out, eyes narrowed in shock. Then, shaking their heads, they stalked back towards the rides, leaving Sophie alone with Zach, the candy-floss suddenly tasting like grit on her tongue.

'Are they your friends?' Zach piped up finally, watching the retreating backs of her so-called best mates. 'Because... you know... They're not really very nice.'

'No,' Sophie snorted. 'I guess they're not really very nice at all...'

'Not like you,' Zach continued, earnest gaze lifting Sophie's leaden heart from its drowning point deep within her chest. 'I think you're the coolest person I know, Sophie. Hey, can we call the phoenix "Sophie" too? You know, when it hatches.'

And that was it, right there, captured in his cheerful, unknowing wisdom. Sophie's black cloud lifted like the smoke wisping from the bonfire's heart of ashes and she laughed, Louise and Debbie and their sickening sixteenth transformation temporarily forgotten in light of Zach's chatter... until Sophie finally felt the truth of his words hit her like the warmth from the flames.

She was cool.

If Louise and Debbie couldn't see what they were missing, who cared? She loved fireworks, reading, basketball, candy-floss, pretending to see phoenix eggs in the free-range egg box with Zach... And it *was* cool – because she didn't want to hide any of it. Why should she? Things changed; Louise and Debbie were proof of that, and maybe Sophie herself was too... But if she had to choose between laughing with Zach and screaming with all those other fakers...? Well. She knew the answer to that – and always would.

Always.

Huge bangs and whistles snapped their focus up to the night sky, a black backcloth illuminated suddenly in bright ochre and gilt colours as the fireworks exploded to sprinkle the stars with flame-trails. Green, blue, purple, gold, white; the colours shone and sputtered in giant arcs and waterfalls down to the horizon, exploding from one small missile at a time to erupt in showers with colossal booms – the most beautiful sight silhouetted against the darkness of November. All faces in the crowd around them were upturned to the display, with even the adults transported back to childish delight as their eyes sparkled in the flickering lights. Sophie swapped a glance with Zach, whose face was alight as the Catherine wheels began spinning at the base of the football pitch and a fountain of silvery, sherbet-like firework fronds spouted higher and higher in the wake of the rockets shooting above.

Sophie stood with the rest, eyes lifted skyward and chin held high. Cool, always.

And then, without warning, the bonfire – like a flaming throne seated between the flying Catherine wheels – exploded, huge flames streaking up towards the sky, a pyre of smoky black, burning orange and blood red. It stretched and stretched, seemingly trying to burn heaven with its golden fingers – and then, as it began to sink back down in a languid, heaving breath, a second shower of flames shot out, tattooed against the inky black depths of the night. Curling and curving, pirouetting and preening, the flames formed a clear shape, burning and smouldering as the crowd below gasped and pointed and applauded in sheer amazement at the astounding pyrotechnics.

It was a bird – huge wings fashioned of ruby red and gold flecked flaming feathers; its eyes were the deep crimson, ringed in ebony, like the heart of a fire, and the plumage of its tale burned in glowing embers. Above its head, the final cluster of rockets and Chinese dragon explosions whizzed and thundered, shrouding the flaming, flapping bird in a shower of rainbow sparks; smoking, it journeyed ever higher, head aimed skyward towards the stars, the horizon, the world...

Sophie stared at the phoenix open-mouthed; beside her, Zach beamed and waved a hand ecstatically up at the disappearing sight.

'See! I *told* you it was a phoenix egg!'

'I – I –' Words failed her, but Zach didn't seem to notice, finger tracing the fire-bird's progress further and further, deeper and deeper, into the night, trailing a tail of flame like a shooting star across the sky. His voice rang out above everything else; excited, full of life and, above all, so, *so* unknowingly wise.

    'Isn't it the coolest thing you ever saw? *Sophie*!'

Ace and Noah

From the day Noah met Ace, there had been problems where food was concerned.

It always proved to be an issue; whenever Noah placed his food within feet of his dog, the dish would immediately be in danger. There had been countless times wherein food had gone missing - whether or not Noah was present at the time was of no consequence. Ace simply didn't care.

The most famous incident amongst Noah and his friends was the night he had finally got Hazel from the office to come over for dinner. The chicken that had been marinating overnight in a sauce - almost impossible to perfect - had been left on the counter, waiting to be placed into the oven... Only to be swallowed whole by one naughty dog. Noah reflected that the plate would have gone too if Ace had been able to get his teeth into it.

Ace never left Noah's side, though. Despite mischievous behaviour, and Noah's tendency to bring young ladies back to his flat after vodka soaked nights out, the two understood one another.

Noah had met Ace by chance. Perhaps, in retrospect, Ace had known what he had been doing all along. He had snuck in through the rickety back door that never quite clicked shut, back when Noah had lived in student accommodation. That was a good four years ago, and through feeding the stray red setter cheap dog food and scraps from the table, a bond was formed.

Which was why today had been so nightmarish.

Ace had disappeared during his walk; become a distant rusty orange dot amongst the green of distant fields, and Noah had shouted and shouted. What was his one bedroom, lacking-in-character flat without his beloved Ace?

It wasn't difficult for panic to set in when your best friend popped out of your life like a rogue bulb or missing house key. Noah extensively searched anywhere and everywhere in proximity to his home, his voice growing higher and more strained with panic each time he called his dog's name. This couldn't be happening, it just couldn't. He couldn't live without his dog, he couldn't bear it.

…Until the fortunate moment that Ace did return. The relief had been more painful than weightless, but Noah had accepted it, and moved on. It wasn't worth thinking more on the matter. His dog was safe and sound after all.

In theory, the problems should have ended there, in the frustrated reunion by the front door of Noah's grotty block of flats – sweaty, red faced owner greeting filthy dog - one hugging and swearing, the other wagging an excited tail against the floor.

The problems should have ended there – but in fact, that was where they started.

"I thought we understood each other," Noah muttered, rubbing his fingers between Ace's ears, the two of them lounged together on the sagging leather sofa; TV blaring, unfinished dinner abandoned on the coffee table. "You broke the trust today, Ace."

Ace groaned in return, a sound that, while animalistic, was laced with regret. Said groan was followed by a hard, throaty cough, and Noah pulled a face.

"No need to overdo it."

Ace coughed again, and his tongue lolled, teeth bared. Something caught in his throat? Noah sat up, a concerned frown knitting his eyebrows together. "Have you been sneaking chicken bones out of the bin again?"

Again, Ace groaned, but impatiently, and Noah firmly took hold of the dog's snout, prising his jaws open to peer down into the black gummed depths of Ace's throat; nothing to see and yet as Noah inspected, Ace wretched, and gave a heavy, honking cough. Something wasn't right.

It only took one sleepless night of overheard choking hacks for Noah to make an executive decision.

*

"We got the X-rays back," the vet explained a week later, when Noah and Ace had returned for the results. The coughing had subsided since, but something was still wrong.

Noah leaned against the vet's table, cold against his back, while Ace sat atop it, leaning against him for support and warmth. Noah's fingers distractedly tangled themselves in the dog's fur as the vet spoke, in a terribly stern voice that made Noah feel like he was back at school.

"See this?" The very-serious-vet tapped the ghostly print of Ace's insides and Noah squinted. There was something in Ace's stomach: small like an eraser and obviously out of place.

"What is-" He began, only for the very-serious-vet to talk over him in an authoritative voice that had no place in a veterinary practise.

"It looks like a memory stick, or USB drive. Why would your dog have eaten such a thing, Mr Parks?"

Noah's face screwed up in confusion, and he turned his bemused stare onto Ace, who wagged his tail – heavy thumps on the sterile table. He sounded amused and Noah scowled.

"It's not funny."

"The coughing was because the drive lodged itself in Ace's throat. Thankfully it wasn't large enough to cause a major issue, but now that's it's reached the bowels, it's causing-"

"I keep all my USB drives in a drawer," Noah insisted, taking the moment to gain some control by interrupting. He knew what he said was fact. He owned three USB drives. One for boring work presentations, one for film scripts he'd never finish, and one for... private entertainment. The vet rolled his eyes, clearly of the opinion already that Noah was an inconsiderate kid, who enjoyed force feeding his dog USB drives. Ace bristled, sensing the attitude, but Noah gave the scruff of his neck a soothing tug.

The vet held up a slip of paper between two fingers.

"Laxatives," he said, eyes betraying just how bored he was of the situation, "should send the drive straight out."

"Yeah, thanks," Noah muttered, snatching the paper. Ace sniffed it and licked his owner's hand. As they headed towards the desk, Noah tried to think how Ace could have got to one of his USB sticks, why he had eaten it at all, and as well as that, which one it was.

That's when it happened.

Down the corridor, there was the distinct sound of doors slamming open, the squeak of boots on tiled floor. Noah glanced up and Ace's ears twitched.

"There it is! That's the one!"

Instantly, Ace shrunk back, sliding behind Noah's legs, his tail tucked beneath him. The body language wasn't difficult to understand. Something was wrong, very wrong. More wrong than swallowed USB sticks and arrogant vets.

Ahead, two enormous men thundered into view, so bulked up with muscle they nearly filled the corridor when stood side by side. Other people and their animals recoiled – cats screeched in alarm, dogs claws skittered against tiling, voices called to one another in shock and confusion. For a moment,

Noah felt as though it was only him and the two invading thugs, with him standing in between them and Ace.

"Get it!"

There was no doubt they were talking about Ace, and there was no doubt that Ace knew why. Spinning on his heel, Noah went to gather up his dog – all four long blundering limbs and shaggy tail – but there was a sharp tug on his hood, sending him careering back before he had a chance.

"Out of the way," a voice snarled down his ear; before Noah could question it, a sharp blow took him out from behind and pain exploded in the back of his head. At a gangly six foot, Noah didn't deal with physical confrontation well, and so he dropped, dazed.

He was aware of the men stepping over him, he was aware of the loud, desperate shriek of Ace as he was scooped up into unkind arms, and it was then that he tried to stand, wobbling legs threatening to give out as he used the wall for support. Down the corridor, the men retreated, hardly giving Noah a second thought, which was perhaps their first mistake.

Shaking away the blurring in the corners of his vision and the dull throb in his head, Noah took off after Ace's captors, wading his way through the chaos of an upended veterinary surgery and out into the car park, where a cliché van waited.

In the heat of the moment, Noah scarcely thought about what was happening, why the men wanted Ace. He only knew that he had to get him back. The morning sunshine was a welcome slap in the face and Noah's balance returned, his vision clearing. It would certainly make driving easier.

Staggering to the car, keys in hand, Noah unlocked it and leapt in. The engine roared to life, just as the reflected van slid by in the rear view mirror. The car reversed, Noah slammed it in gear, and then he was off, rocketing to the most bizarre rescue.

He drove, keeping up with the van ahead, hardly caring that the men would know they were being followed, and by the gawky twenty-something they had punched, too. Noah tried to rearrange his thoughts into something that made sense. Had this been some kind of raid for suitable dogs to sell on? Noah knew that dogs were often stolen, but he wondered why his red setter with the questionable pedigree would be so appealing.

It should have struck him then: Ace had recently disappeared and he had swallowed something unusual, but that thought didn't come to Noah as he drove, despite his thinking that he had a solid handle on the motives of his dog's kidnappers. All he could think about was what if he lost them? What if he never saw Ace again? There would be no more companionable meals together, no more walks in rain or sun, no more slobbering wake up calls, no more wet kisses, no more wet dog. At this thought, Noah's foot absently pressed down harder on the accelerator, to a point where he was rather obviously bumper to bumper with the van in front.

Noah obviously still wasn't a threat. The van accelerated with an enormous growl, and took off down the quiet road. Noah tried to follow, but there

252

was more than a slight difference between a beaten up Ford Polo and a hulking great Volkswagen with an engine probably bigger than Noah himself. He realised, with a sinking feeling, that he'd never catch up.

He drummed his fingers on the wheel, tapping out a frustrated rhythm as he thought. Stout houses shot by, trees lining their fronts like guards, and Noah thought, and he thought... He walked Ace along these streets every day - fond memories, precious time together.

His eyes flickered back to the distant van. They wouldn't be from this quiet suburb, they'd be making their way back to the main road, out of the minute town and back into the city. Noah knew this place better than them, better than anyone.

Surrounding them was the Dickens estate – roads quaintly named after characters – and Noah flashed back to midnight walks or morning strolls with Ace, enjoying one another's company as they made their way down Micawber Road, or Copperfield, Curzon, Pickwick... It was a tiny, literary maze, and if Noah took the right turns he'd beat Ace's captors to the main road, no problem.

In that second of realisation, Noah jerked the wheel and the Ford took a sharp turn left, and into the jungle.

A right on Micawber, another hard right down Tapley, swinging left up Marley, down Copperfield and...

Noah brought the Ford out onto Dickens Lane and, behind him, the van slammed on its brakes, horn blaring in warning. Noah stared in his rear view mirror, chest heaving, adrenaline pumping. He could see the figure of one of the men in the front seat, hunched forward, eyes narrowed. Idly, Noah flicked the locks on his car door.

There was silence; a painful waiting silence that expected something to happen.

No car doors flew open, no booted feet came stomping towards Noah. Instead, the engine flared once more, and the van roared forward, circling the muddy little Ford and taking off down the road. Immediately, Noah put his foot down, and the chase began again, this time evenly as the two cars hit traffic.

Noah had never been so pleased to see morning rush hour traffic in his life. If the van was stationary, this would be his only chance to do anything, and so Noah veered off, bumping up onto the pavement where he killed the engine. He took the crook lock from beneath the passenger seat and weighed it in his hands. It'd do for a weapon, not that Noah was sure he'd have the confidence to wield it. He just knew he'd die trying to save Ace, no matter what reason it was that he was stolen, and Noah clung to this thought as he ran into the road, took hold of the back doors of the van and wrenched them open.

A copper head looked up from the confines of a dog crate and a familiar flame-licked tail began to wag. Ace would always be pleased to see Noah, regardless of the situation, which at that moment happened to be a dark van interior, not much different to the insides of a tuna tin, with the largest, potentially most terrifying man Noah had ever come across, guarding him.

"Leave well enough alone, mate," the thug warned, in a voice edged with threat. He rose from his seat, approaching with meaty, clenched fists. "It's just a dog."

"Ace is not just a dog," Noah corrected, and he bravely hitched himself up onto the back of the van, one trembling hand gripping the open door, the other, rather ridiculously, brandishing the crook lock.

As if on cue, the van set off, the suddenness sending Noah stumbling forward, weapon skidding across the floor of the van and colliding with Ace's cage with a clang that whirred in his ears. He tried to right himself, but the van sped up, despite the open back doors, and Noah found he could hardly stand, let alone keep his balance.

"Give him back to me," he warned, trying to arrange himself against the back wall so that he at least looked somewhat threatening. The doors flapped open and closed, cold morning wind rushed inside the confines of the van and blew Noah's hair around his face in whips of orange. The bottleneck of rush hour traffic dispersed as they moved onto a quieter, more suburban street, leaving Noah struggling to remain upright as they picked up speed.

"It's not the dog we want, it's what it's swallowed!" Came the reply, and Noah blinked as the penny dropped.

Ace had vanished, had obviously come across some sort of meeting... Their walk earlier in the week had been on one of the hottest days of the year, could Ace have invaded some form of illegitimate picnic, gobbled up several sandwiches and a fallen USB drive on the way? He didn't want to think about how the men were planning on retrieving the drive itself, nor what was on it exactly, he just knew now that the stakes were doubled... and already they had been high.

In the distance Noah could hear – with relief - the whine of police sirens and he figured it made sense, considering how they were driving, and just how despicably dangerous it all was.

The van was careering down a road with speed bumps now, each one it hit sending violent hiccups through the entire vehicle: if Noah had struggled with his balance before, now it was just impossible. His main plan was to not fall out of the back doors and into the road, and from what he could gather, the thug he shared the tin box with had the same idea. Ace, meanwhile, was whipping his head back and forth, his gaze mainly resting on Noah in concern, as his clawed feet gained as much purchase on the floor of the crate as possible.

How did he plan on dealing with this when the van eventually came to a stop? He was outnumbered, Ace was locked away and god knows where the crook lock had gone now.

The sirens had become louder, so close they may well have been on top of the van itself, and Noah glanced back to see, with a heart that sung, that the police were tailing them closely. Up front, one of thugs swore, and took a sharp turn, swerving abruptly down the next street – only to hit an oncoming car, front bumper to headlight.

Noah was certain he'd suffer from car sickness forever after that, as the van swung around, spinning and screeching, out of control, until a lamppost stood in its path and stopped it dead with a deafening crunch: a giant fist taking out a metal monster. Noah was flung against the wall of the van, the air sucked out of him by powerful hands, and he sank to the floor, crumpled and winded.

The sirens had stopped, but through his closed eyes, Noah could feel and see the pulse of electric blue as the lights blared with brightness. One part of Noah's brain insisted that it needed a moment, and his body agreed, but another part of him - louder, more passionate - screamed 'Ace' again and again, and the strength came to him, and Noah began to stand, dragging himself up by the steel bars of the crate that held his best friend. There was no sound from him, no tell-tale groan or thump of tail, and Noah fought back the rise of panic as he tried to gather his bearings.

His vision cleared and Noah's brain began to catch up, reminding him that this was the second time he had taken an injury to the head, and it most certainly wasn't happy about it. Noah ignored that for the moment – ignored everything, even the call of the officers, and the murmured demand for backup.

When he finally focused, Ace's form came into view: those copper licks of fur, wet mushroom nose and eyes that showed far more emotion than they were given credit for. More importantly, those

257

eyes were open, and the tail was slowly building up a wag. In a second, Noah had unlatched the door to the cage and Ace bounded out, unharmed, having been protected by the bars. He wriggled into Noah's arms like sausage meat forcing itself into a skin, soft grunts and whines escaping his throat as he welcomed his best friend and rescuer.

"You're okay, you're okay," was all Noah could manage, his fingers delving into shaggy hair, tugging on ridiculous ears, while his nose met with a desperately licking tongue. They knew one another inside out, Ace and Noah, and together they told one another how pleased they were to be reunited, and just how terrible those questionable moments had been.

*

With alibis like the veterinary surgery – including the unlikely hero in the form of very-serious-vet – Noah and Ace were cleared quickly of any charges, but were directed to appear in court as witnesses. Or at least Noah was.

The USB drive turned up just over a week later, which was an unpleasant experience for both dog and owner and something Noah wished they hadn't made a point of on the cover of the daily rag newspaper. They had inevitably covered the story of the naughty dog and his hero owner, helping to catch two criminals known for working extensively in the black market.

Noah was given orders by the police to take the memory stick to headquarters as soon as it made an appearance - but, Noah argued with himself, they didn't have to know that he had looked at it beforehand... Did they? These were the thoughts that flicked through his mind as he sat on the sagging sofa, in his usual position, Ace leaning on him, the two even more inseparable since the incident.

"Right then, Ace, just one look, and then its marinated chicken for the two of us, yeah?"

Ace gave a familiar groan of approval, and Noah shoved the drive into the USB slot. There was a beat, the computer whirred, and then the file opened up in the form of a white square with one tiny yellow file to show for it.

Noah scratched between Ace's ears distractedly and took a deep breath, before giving the file a double click. What was the worst that could happen? Secret government files would bounce across his screen, giving Noah information he barely understood? Schematics for military aircrafts? Proof that aliens existed, and the Roswell incident had indeed been a cover up?

It was very exciting, yes; potentially more exciting than Ace and Noah's latest adventure. As long as he didn't copy the files, nobody needed to know and, Noah justified, who in their right mind wouldn't investigate a much sought after USB treasure trove?

There was nothing wrong with a little curiosity.

Self-Portrait, in Charcoal and Tears

Darling Ella,

Lying beside me now, your tiny face is screwed up in the concentration of sleep. I draw you every day. But art can't express the memories I suddenly need to relive, or bring back the woman – closer than my own lost mother – who changed my life and helped found the moments that led me to you.

Neither can it show you the precious things that she taught me; things that must, one day, be shared with you.

So, for now, I'll write them here – so that when that day comes, she will touch your life as she did mine.

*

Her name was Rosalynn Carter and the first time I met her, I was barely seventeen. I had reached that point in growing up where every focus is suddenly turned to what will come next and how you will walk successfully down life's glittering paths of opportunity.

For me, art was my only talent; I had always had a sharp, keen sense of the ephemeral, a knack for capturing a fleeting expression or a stolen second... Only, after I impetuously cast all other professions aside, my gift suddenly began to fail me.

And so my art teacher recommended I visit Rosalynn.

She had been a portrait artist in the '50s, with famous exhibits that people flocked to see. But then unappreciative 'modern art' sprung up, photography outdid portraiture – and Rosalynn Carter's star dimmed, flickered hazily for a moment, and then went out.

Only history reincarnated her; flying back through the years to reignite her once-renowned name to the new buds crowding the garden of artistry. The past sucked Ros up and deposited her in the here and now, ensconced within the house of her youth: a huge, towering manor, red-bricked and old-fashioned, with brightly sugared plates of glass bordering the windows and wooden framework everywhere.

I would have been daunted if I knew how my life was about to change, but I didn't really know what that feeling was back then. I had been on my own so much that I simply lived inside my head – always thoughtlessly pressing forward...

*

'So you're the new hopeful.' It wasn't a question; issued at the first opening of that great oak door, Rosalynn stood straight-backed and steely-eyed. Grey hair straggled around canvas skin of

261

fading papyrus – a face creased at the edges, staining coffee-cream. She stepped back, allowing me entry like it was a privilege. 'Well, come in. Let's see what you can do.'

I would be lying if I said I wasn't taken aback. Within minutes, an easel was facing me, a whole array of brushes, paints and pencils at my disposal. The sitting room was all chintz and chiffon. With a flourish, her every movement precise, Rosalynn set a mirror before me.

My portfolio leant, discarded and forgotten, against the front door.

'Draw.'

With that command, Ros seated herself in a chair a little way from me and waited, dark eyes sharp as a hawk's. I cleared my throat uncertainly. Rosalynn sighed.

'How can I assess your potential if I don't see you draw?'

'I – I brought some of my work with me –'

She waved my protests aside with a snort.

'I need to see how your art comes. That's where talent lies. Now: draw.'

'Myself?'

'Who else?' She frowned.

'But –'

'How can you draw others, capture their very heart in their eyes, their face, if you cannot even set your own soul free across the page?'

Somewhat thrown, I hesitantly surveyed my pale, wide-eyed features in the mirror. I looked the picture of blankness, framed by straw-coloured curls. A plain angel. My reflection preened vainly, the person I suddenly wished I was.

With a surge of discontent, I selected a pencil.

*

An hour later, I smudged a last wave into a strand of hair and sat back. The entire, silent time, I had been fully conscious of Ros' eyes upon me, shrewdly attentive, as though mentally painting her own portrait of my character.

I reached for my sketch, but she was already behind me, looming crow-like over my shoulder. I froze, waiting, as her gaze roamed over my work, expert and critical. Then, just as abruptly, she stepped back.

'It's a start. Come back next week. We'll see if we can't progress you further than simply drawing the technical points of what's in front of you.'

My heart plummeted. I ran a glance over my portrait. It was good – better than I had recently been capable of at any rate. Was I really so bad, in her professional opinion?

Something in my expression must have caught Ros' eye, for she sighed wearily, mouth crinkling with disparagement.

'You have potential. You just have to free your talent from your fears.'

The next thing I knew, I was up out of my chair and in front of the door, my portfolio handed to me as though it were a childish plaything.

'Come back next week. We'll try again.'

*

After such an odd introduction, I can't say exactly why I did return the following week. My reception was no different; Rosalynn swept me into the same sitting room, placed the same mirror before me and issued the same instruction. An hour later, I again received the barest compliment of having 'adequate technical skill' before being told to come back next week for another attempt.

Two more weeks passed.

Nothing changed.

By the fifth week, I was certain this was a joke to her.

'I was told you're the best – that you would advise me! So far, Mrs Carter, I've just drawn myself repeatedly, received no comments for improvement and seen nothing of your own work!'

Her commanding self-assurance didn't even falter.

'How can you improve your style by looking at my work?' A sigh. 'You are drawing well, but you are not seeing, girl. Until you can see yourself, truly and without predilections, and show it in your portrait, you will never possess the freedom to capture anyone else as they truly are satisfactorily.'

I had no response. The teacher-pupil back-story I had conjured in my head for when I was famous in future years was rapidly self-destructing. Ros nodded appreciatively at my silence, folding

264

her arms in that wise manner the older generation have unspeakably mastered.

'I do not improve people, child. One day, they simply find themselves. Now come back next week.'

*

Months began to pass. Father went away on business more and more, unable now to look at me; every day that went by simply modelled me into my Mother and it broke his heart. My art faltered massively. Each week, I felt I was tripping ever closer to something, just beyond my reach, and Ros' dismissive attitude to every drawing only made the longing ache worse.

And then that day came – the day my other dream, the one outside of art, came true.

For three years, I had been hideously infatuated with Aaron Dennis, my imagination growing in its loneliness with every school day that whirled past. He would sweep me off my feet at the parties we attended, holding my hand, his hair a golden halo and his words perfect, like him. But, in reality, he'd never noticed me; the plain, abandoned angel.

Except he did.

At Susie Jenkins' eighteenth birthday, the music blaring and the alcohol uninhibited, Aaron Dennis came to me and told me that I was all he wanted. His tall, muscular body in front of me – a dream come true – he was my knight, my hero... The only one to ever want me at all.

Now I realise his talk of love was self-indulgent, his actions simply those of a dare.

Hindsight is a terrible thing, Ella.

That night, he wanted me – a thirty minute doomed romance.

After that night, the last tattered shreds of my self-confidence withered, caving in – and, five weeks after that, something else in me died too.

*

My whole life felt erased. I had always been solitary, but now it crushed me. I continued sessions at Rosalynn's, but I couldn't draw. It was worse than before. Every time I looked in that mirror, all I saw were deadened eyes – no longer even the plain, abandoned, fallen angel. The nothing suddenly revealed in me burnt a ceaseless fire of humiliation – each time I walked to school; saw his cruel face; or saw my own naive, childish reflection.

Sitting in Ros' parlour, charcoal snapped between my fingers.

In the glass, Rosalynn's expression, one that had grown strangely familiar, suddenly softened for the first time. Then – an oracle – she asked me the one question I needed, but could never have expected.

'Why are you so alone, love?'

Her pitying words struck my heart, a painful bullet of undeserved sympathy. I slumped forward onto the table, dye and pastel smearing my face – and I cried. I cried for my foolishness, my shame, my failure... my betrayed, unborn life.

I felt hands on my shoulders, gnarled fingers that would never draw again; my mortification deepened. I was a waste. Then a forehead rested against my lank hair and Ros' voice, unexpectedly soft and maternal, whispered in my ear.

'You wanted to know why I always make you draw yourself? Because you need to stop thinking you are empty, worthless. The face is the entrance to the heart, my love – and the eyes are the windows to the soul. Your eyes told me what you have given up, and I'm afraid it will always scar you. But you don't live through years of fame without realising a few things, so trust an old woman on this: as alone as you may feel right now, it'll get better...'

I clung to her, to her words, tears staining the blank paper beneath us as I howled.

And then, as she smoothed my hair, she spoke words I will never forget – the words that changed my life.

'Someday you will understand, darling – you're free now. Today is the day that you have finally seen yourself.'

*

Six exhibitions and one marriage later, I travelled once again, now heavily pregnant, to Ros' house. Nothing had changed except the flowers trailing the trellises and flowerbeds; it felt like journeying a decade back into the dusty past.

Over the years, Rosalynn never stopped helping me. She held my hand as I stepped into the

267

world, steadily nurtured my talent into bloom and watched encouragingly from afar as I finally stumbled across success – and love.

And she never once admitted her part in it, continually waving away my gratitude. Rosalynn Carter was always adamant: she didn't teach people, didn't help them – they helped themselves. Once, ever-modest, she told me tutoring was simply another artistic project, keeping her busy.

But she couldn't stay busy forever.

The night she went, I held her hand, paper-thin and frail, the face I now knew as well as my own peaceful as she quietly slipped away. From that first second, I missed her more than I could stand.

In the following weeks, as I cleared through her memories, I came across a room I had never been in before. Sunlight streamed in through a wall of bay windows, dappling the huge array of portraits that lined the room. For a minute, I thought they were Rosalynn's own works, until I remembered she had donated every last one to galleries the world over.

Then I realised.

The faces gazing down at me, warm, full of life, were all the souls Ros always claimed she "hadn't" healed; the people she "hadn't" helped. In their eyes, I could see that streak of happiness that only comes from her touch. My throat hurt, and I pressed a hand to my stomach, wanting you, Ella, to share in this final moment with Ros.

Because there – central amid the faces – was me.

And I was smiling.

Foreign Terrain

The world of Ikea is almost entirely separate from ours.

A mad labyrinth of amputated bedrooms and bathrooms, secret passages and narrow walkways; people jovially walking down them, hardly knowing their way at all, hardly caring where the arrows on the pathways could take them.

The world of household furniture and crockery is a strange one.

Lucy considered all of this as she wandered through the shop in search of necessities for her new home - making a point of sitting on beds, lifting the lids on desks and pushing herself along on desk chairs.

'Do you actually know what you're looking for?' Asked Charlotte, the friend she had dragged along with her. She traipsed after the bright freckled face of Lucy, who occasionally tossed a snarl of light brown hair away from her eyes so that she could see prices better.

'Things, you know, grown up things. For the flat.'

Charlotte folded her arms.

'We've got the basics. You don't need to start worrying about desk chairs and plant pots until we're fully moved in.'

'Well isn't that what people do when they move out of their house for the first time? They go to Ikea. They buy loads of houseware, and then spend hours putting them together. Then they begin working nine 'til five, realising that this really is it...' Lucy had paused, staring at the reflected world, distorted in a collection of oddly shaped mirrors on the wall opposite. Charlotte pressed her lips together and stood by her.

'You don't have to move in if you don't want to. Sarah says she's had enough of living with her dad, and she'd be happy to-'

'No,' Lucy smiled, shaking her head. 'No, sorry. I'm just not used to the idea. New terrain, y'know! Bedside tables - that's what we need. Well, I need one. To put books on, mainly,' and she wandered off once more, into the depths of the shop.

'Well I'll look at lamps then, yeah? Meet you at the cafe in-' Charlotte paused, realising Lucy was not listening, and probably would not listen to her at all during the preparation for the move. She waved her hand dismissively and set off in the other direction.

*

Lucy didn't really want any of the things Ikea had to offer. She didn't like the idea of buying all of this new, sterile furniture to replace the wardrobes and chests of drawers she identified with home. Did she really want to move? Was that what this was about? Was she really worried that living

271

like an 'adult' would mean she suddenly became boring?

She was in her early twenties. She had years and years of partying and adventuring left in her, but would leading a nine to five life suddenly make her mundane?

She stopped, leant against one of the surrounding dining room tables and sighed. Ikea was too large and vast for her. She had been roaming for some time in search of the bedside tables, and so far every table but the one she had desired had turned up.

Ikea wasn't as fun as they made it look on '500 Days of Summer.' After the first couple of visits, it lost all charm and just became one vast warehouse of soulless items, waiting to be homed, or built...

What little charm remained, came in the form of specified paths, which weren't the necessary ways to escape the shop itself. A variety of hidden passages ran between sections, bringing you out in places you didn't know existed. It was those that Lucy intended to find and make use of, so she wouldn't get lost amongst the madness, (or lack thereof).

Feeling along the walls, smirking at her own personal homage to 'Labyrinth', Lucy wondered how long it would take her to get back to the cafe if she shot through each hidden nook. Perhaps she'd tumble into an oubliette, or face off against the Goblin King while she was at it...

Her hand slipped, and she stumbled forward, against the corner of the wall leading to the adjacent passage. Releasing a grunt of irritation, Lucy straightened up and faced the opening full on before hurrying down it without looking forward or back- afraid somebody might have seen her clumsy display.

It was after a few seconds of walking, staring with pink cheeks at her feet, that Lucy began to wonder where she was. Her footfalls were alarmingly loud and echoed against walls that should not have been tall enough to have such an effect - and when she finally looked up, only black surrounded her.

There was equal darkness ahead and, after one swift glance back the way she had come, she found the same scene behind.

Perhaps all of the lights in the shop had gone out? Perhaps if she carried on straight forward, she would find other people. Perhaps the lights would have come back on by then...

She quickened her pace, frightened now, desperate; she wondered where Charlotte was, if she was alright, if everyone else in the shop was alright...

Lucy's foot brushed against what felt like rubble, rolling and crunching under foot. Snapping her gaze up, she saw a vast, green landscape stretching out before her, pinpricks of colour dotted in the distance- wild flowers growing. She looked down, and flinched away when she saw where she was standing- on the edge of a verge, angling down sharply.

'Oh my God,' she staggered back, whirling, confused and lost, only to see that the corridor no longer followed her. A further expanse of grass was there instead, soft and fluffy in appearance – definitely not the squeaky plastic floor of Ikea.

Lucy quite simply didn't understand. She had been looking for bedside tables, and then...And then this?

It made no sense.

'Hello?' She called, her voice instantly torn away by a wind that picked up all around her. She pulled her anorak close, looking left and right.

'Hello!'

The voice that replied was cheerful, distinctly male, and Lucy span around, having flinched in surprise at the sound.

A young man leapt back at her sudden movement, raising his hands in a surrender which Lucy thought to be quite unnecessary.

'Sorry!' He smiled at her, keeping a safe distance. 'I didn't mean to make you jump. I just got excited, that's all!'

'I got lost,' replied Lucy, keeping her eyes on him. 'Could you point me in the direction of Ikea?'

She wasn't calm, not at all. The words fell from her mouth with a life of their own, telling her how to feel and forcing her outwardly to stick to that. Inside, a fierce shudder was threatening to dance up and down her legs and arms. If such a thing happened, she would most likely fall from the cliff. She took a wary step away from the edge.

'I'm Toby.' He thrust his hand out, looking guilty. 'There isn't an Ikea near here. Well, not anymore. The Gap comes out all over the place. This was one of the more unfortunate locations.'

Lucy eyed him, and then took his hand.

'Riiight…'

Toby pumped her hand with great enthusiasm, for so long and with such excitement, that Lucy had to struggle free.

'Is this a science thing? Parallel dimensions and stuff? I watch 'Doctor Who', I know about these things…' She was trying to be rational. Despite not being the sort of person who involved herself in the adult world willingly, Lucy was trying to look at everything from a logical view point. She had been in Ikea, and then she was there. That was a fact. What was also a fact was that Toby's constant grin was beginning to frustrate her.

'Will you stop smiling?' She snapped suddenly, picking this as the thing that would bother her, out of everything that was happening. 'You aren't helping! You're not helping at all!'

Toby's face fell.

'Sorry.'

For the first time, Lucy actually looked at him. He was younger than her, but not by that much - a couple of years perhaps. When you were in your twenties, though, one or two made all the difference. He had brown hair, which was long and creeping below his ears. His fringe was combed to one side in a scruffy manner - Toby was obviously not the sort of person who liked keeping it under control, but had to. It looked as though it had been 'neatened' with some haste. His jaw was quite angular, but his features were soft. He wore a black zipper jacket, with a strange logo on the breast. It certainly wasn't the Ikea logo, and Lucy stared at it for a questioning few moments.

Toby hadn't noticed, and was too busy explaining his excitement at Lucy's sudden appearance. He couldn't seem to restrain himself.

'They told me in the induction you know! They said 'Toby, when you close the gaps, it's possible you might get a Wanderer. But it doesn't happen often. Just close the gap as quick as poss-'' He paused, and frowned, noticing Lucy's curiosity. 'What's the matter?'

'The logo on your jacket,' Lucy straightened up. 'What is it?'
'It's the logo for the company I work for.' He looked wistful, and Lucy thought he must finally have noticed the questions she had forced down, and her general confusion.

'Do you want to go somewhere? I'll explain things. Then maybe we can get you back to your Ikea.'

*

They had been walking for some time, through what Lucy could only describe as wasteland. The cliff had disappeared long behind them and given way to sandpaper like ground, reaching far and flat, seemingly infinite.

Neither of them had said a word, but as the scenery rolled by, featuring nothing but distant hills and nearer, dusty flat ground, Lucy grew impatient.

'My name's Lucy, but you called me a Wanderer. Why?'

Toby looked over at her.

'That's what they call you, down at the office,' he cleared his throat. 'I'm quite new. I should really check the protocols for this. I know there's something I should be remembering, something really important about Wanderers. You're not supposed to be running around in foreign terrains, but there's a reason behind that...' He frowned, and slid a hand into his back pocket. Swiftly, he removed a journalist's notepad from the confines and began flipping through the pages.

'I had to write everything down,' he explained, rather haphazardly, as he flicked one page after another. 'There's a lot of stuff to - Oh! Here it is!' He opened his mouth to speak, and as if in answer, a gunshot tore through the air.

Lucy squeaked in alarm, and whirled in the direction of the sound, despite her better judgement. Toby had gone rigid, but was already facing that direction, notepad clutched in one hand, other curled into a fist.

'Did he just shoot at us?' Lucy demanded, staring in panic at the man who stood a short distance away.

He wore shades, which he lowered with a grin that twitched and tugged menacingly at the corner of his mouth. He reminded Lucy of the maniacal faces that sneered at her from the television during Crimewatch, and a shudder skittered down her spine as a result.

The pistol in his hand shone in the bright daylight.

'...Warning shot.' Murmured Toby distractedly, keeping his eyes fixed on the man, who continued smiling like he was in on a joke nobody else knew the punch line to.

'Let the Wanderer come right on over to me, and the next shot won't be aimed to kill.' His voice had a smooth drawl Lucy couldn't quite understand. She swallowed thickly, already confused, but now frightened as well. This couldn't be having a positive effect on her health.

'That was it,' hissed Toby, only loud enough for Lucy to hear. She wanted to look at him, but she held her gaze on their assailant - and his weapon. 'Bounty hunters. I haven't even had a chance to...' He swore and held the small notepad tighter in his hand. 'There aren't many Wanderers, so there aren't many bounty hunters, but they can sniff you out, they can-'

'I haven't got all day, kid.' The bounty hunter strode forward, the buckles on his boots clinking and tinkling. 'I haven't had a Wanderer in months. Funds are running a little low.'

'I'm a Wanderer - I walked in here without being invited...is that it? I only...I only wanted some stuff for my flat, I...Why? Why...' Lucy shook her head, trying to tie together some of her loose thoughts so that they made at least an inch of sense. All the while the man in black approached, and with each step he took, Lucy shuffled nearer to Toby - her only protection. 'Why didn't you know? Why weren't you trying to-'

'I'm new.' replied Toby with some force. 'This was the first day they left me on my own. This is my luck, this is my luck all over...' He turned to her and took her hand in his. 'If he gets you, I'm sacked. RUN!'

They turned and bolted, but if it had not been for Toby's fierce tugging on her hand, Lucy would never have run. People with weapons should not be fled from: they should be given what they want, to avoid the shooting. That had always been Lucy's philosophy, at least.

As if to emphasise her thoughts, another gunshot resounded behind them, cutting through the air. Lucy screamed and stumbled, covering her head with her spare hand. To her left, she saw a chunk of hardened gravel explode into a small mushroom of sand and dust as the bullet made contact with it.

Shrieking, she staggered and suddenly released Toby's hand, rather than holding onto it tighter.

He called her name, but Lucy ran. She ran hard and fast, desperate to find somewhere, anywhere, that made more sense than here. She wanted to believe she was having some kind of episode - she would take that over being shot at any day, but an un-ignorable part of her knew that this was all very real.

The landscape was flat, but as she ran, listening to the roars of anger from the bounty hunter, she noticed on the horizon bright white rocks of curious shapes and sizes, silhouetted against the sunset. She made for them now, so focused on her goal that she tuned out the sounds from behind her. She hardly noticed the sudden lack of gunshots as she arrived in the strange jungle of odd shapes - which she finally realised was not dotted with rocks after all.

Chairs, tables, lamps...Every piece of household furniture one could think of was splayed around her, creating a jungle much more chaotic than the average Ikea, but also not dissimilar. Lucy slowed to view her strange surroundings: just as her hand reached out, to touch a desk chair tipped on it's side, she snapped back to the matter at hand - and promptly leapt behind a bureau. She couldn't hear Toby, or their terrifying attacker, and she was too scared to look. The eerie silence scared her more than the gun shots ever could, and she wrapped her arms around herself – feeling safer for it.

There she stayed, breathing in and out, chest rising and falling in her panic. Lucy brushed her hair from her face, cradled her cheeks in clammy hands and began to cry. She cried for her sanity, for the changes she was forcing herself into, for the sense that none of this made, and that she so wished it did.

Like any moment of realisation, Lucy's came at the strangest and most inconvenient of times; on her own, leaning against a bureau in an Ikea wasteland, hiding from a bounty hunter who wanted her for being in the wrong place at the wrong time.

Why had she been in Ikea in the first place? Purchasing items to represent a change she wasn't yet ready for? Totems to place around an unloved and unhappy flat? She lifted her face up, and her eyes took in the furniture that surrounded her once more. Bedside tables tipped on their heads - pots for plants that didn't need watering and so served no point - desks with drawers and pockets that would go unused – and, of course, wall sconces and patterned dustpans and brushes - pointless decorations to enhance the average.

Her juddering cries ceased slowly, and she sniffed. The tears stuck to her cheeks like cling film, thickened by her mascara, and so she wiped them, letting out the occasional pitiful gasp.

No, Lucy realised slowly. She didn't need to change, not until she was ready.

She stood up suddenly, so sure of herself in that second that she had forgotten entirely where she was. Spinning around, Lucy saw, a short distance away now, Toby and the bounty hunter, grappling. One of the younger man's hands was wrapped around the hunter's, preventing him from pulling the trigger of the weapon. No punches had been thrown, and would not be thrown, not while the possession of the gun was in question.

'You Stitchers are all the same. Useless! What good is it going to do, sending the Wanderers back? We'll only end up with more of that crap, the furniture that leaks through. Why don't you send that back, hm?' There was a tinge to the voice of the Hunter that twisted Lucy's stomach uncomfortably. She had a strong feeling that he was capable of so much more than he let on.

She took a lamp in hand, tossed it from palm to palm and strode bravely towards the two men. All eyes went to her, and the struggles turned to tension as they held onto each other tightly and watched Lucy approach. It was only her who could break them apart.

'Let him go,' Lucy snarled, raising the lamp as threateningly as she could manage. The Hunter looked startled at first, but then he grinned – that was more unnerving.

'Oh, alright then, Wanderer.' He threw Toby away from him suddenly, wrenching the gun from his grasp in the process. Toby whirled and stumbled, staggering to a halt against Lucy, who looked him over.

'Are you alright?'

There was the click of a loaded gun, causing Toby and Lucy to look up. The weapon was aimed right at them, so close they were staring right down the barrel.

In that second, Lucy endeavoured to make the quickest decision of her life. She tightened her hands around the neck of the lamp, and swung it low, dipping her entire body so that she was beneath the nose of the gun. There was a bang as it fired, the sound mixing simultaneously with the thud of ceramic to stomach. Lucy was sure she felt the short breath of wind from the bullet whipping through the air, tickle the top of her head, just slightly. Detailed dreams.

The Hunter lurched backwards, released a pained grunt and fell to the floor, horribly winded. Lucy dropped the now mostly shattered lamp and looked to Toby.

'It'd be nice to know where I saw you in real life. I heard once that our brain picks up the image of a person and places them into your dreams. I'd like to thank you.'

Toby gave her a bemused look; one that Lucy was sure wasn't visible simply because she had surprised him.

'Usually Wanderers just stagger about, bumping into things.' He looked down at the Hunter, who was holding his stomach, eyes tight shut. His sunglasses lay at the side of his head, having skittered away in the collision. 'That's what they told me, anyway. Maybe they were lying.'

Lucy nodded slowly, amused by him, surveying the surroundings casually now.

'So where is this supposed to be, anyway?'

'This is the wastelands,' replied Toby. 'It's where most of the gaps come out, for some reason, and so the Hunters swarm here.'

'They've not got much to do with their time then,' commented Lucy, noticing less and less the smells in the air, and the feel of the light breeze in her long hair. Even Toby was looking less solid. The world was fading. She narrowed her eyes and observed him closely as he continued.

'Wanderers aren't sighted often, and if they are? They'd make millions parading someone like you around.'

Lucy nodded slowly, understanding now. The reality of the situation oozed into her subconscious, coming through the gates with great ease as other weights lifted themselves from her mind.

'I thought other worlds were supposed to be.... I don't know, nice and different.' She said, slightly pensive.

'Sorry to disappoint you. A tear in the fabric of reality can destroy civilisations... because people are greedy.' Toby ran a hand through his hair and let out an exasperated huff.

'People *are* greedy,' agreed Lucy. 'Can you get me back, yet? I have stuff to do.' She glanced around at the overturned furniture, cluttering and surrounding them, and a smile curled her lips into a Cupid's bow. 'Stuff I've finally got around to understanding.'

'Don't get too excited, it's only a parallel world,' Toby replied, deadpan. Lucy's expression forced him to check himself, and he hastily gestured to their surroundings- to the chairs, the madness. 'Funnily enough, the new gap's come out here.' He pulled something from his pocket, and with bemusement, Lucy saw it was a yo-yo.

'Really? Really? A yo-yo? You're just being silly now.'

'It's the best way to find the gaps, and it's fun. You've got to get your kicks somewhere.' He rolled it out of his hand, the string extended, and the yo-yo tumbled towards the ground. Toby tipped his hand this way and that, the toy bouncing up and down, and he looked towards Lucy with a childish smile. 'Can you do tricks?'

Lucy shook her head. 'I haven't played with a yo-yo in years.'

'You should,' Toby replied absently, flicking it forward. It leaped through the air, still anchored by the string. 'This one's called 'around the world', but if there's a portal nearby, it never gets that far.'

As if to back up Toby's point, the yo-yo paused mid-air, the string looped around it pulled taut. It quivered, an unseen force tugging on it with all it's might. Lucy's eyes widened.

'You weren't kidding.'

'In my line of work, you can't kid.' Toby gestured casually ahead of them. 'Go back through, and I'll close it behind you.'

Lucy took a couple of hesitant steps forward, ducking past the hovering yo-yo, and she turned one last time, with a slight frown on her face.

'Surely you'd have a right job, cleaning this wasteland of 'Wanderers'? Ikea is full of these portals, right?'

Toby shrugged in reply, looking far more casual than Lucy would have expected.

'You'd be surprised how many people follow the outlined tracks in Ikea; why do you think they make them in the first place? Even they don't trust the fabric of reality. A place like Ikea is bound to have a Narnia or two. Too many wardrobes.'

Lucy nodded slowly. These were the present facts, even if they were beginning to blur around the edges. The fading world had brought her an epiphany, something she had never thought would come to her in Ikea, or even in a parallel wasteland at the close of a chase.

'And you're going to stitch this up when I'm gone? This portal?'

'Getting you back is the stitch.' Toby reeled in the yo-yo, catching it in his open hand suddenly. He wrapped the string back around it as he spoke. 'So you're kind of the Stitcher, here.'

Lucy looked back to the supposed location of the doorway between worlds. She was sure she could see the air ripple just slightly, not dissimilar to the quiver of air as gas rises. She should have been frightened to go back, to return with her new frame of mind, her new understanding of her own wants and needs, but she couldn't find it in her. Lucy wasn't scared at all.

'You never know,' she said, without turning back, taking another step towards the portal which sandwiched between two desk chairs. 'I might wander off the path again sometime.'

'I'll be here.' Toby answered brightly from behind her. 'But I think you're quite good at doing it alone.'

Lucy knew she was, and that was her final thought as she stepped between worlds, and emerged on the other side.

Thank you to...

Our families,
for coping with our mad ramblings

James,
our glorious cover artist and supportive guru

Sam,
for invaluable advice

And to Neil Gaiman and Stephen King,
who inspired us to start writing in the first place

About the Authors

Jenny and Victoria have been friends for over a decade now, bonded by a love of cake and of course, stories.

Jenny has an HND in media production, but ran away to sell toys and write novels after being expected to learn about the inside of televisions. Victoria, meanwhile, has worked in and around books since her mid-teens; she devours books like biscuits and now wants to write them too – surprising.

Most of their stories are set in their fair city of Manchester, which they believe does not get enough literary credit. They both have brown hair and glasses, but are definitely not sisters – stop asking.

Printed in Great Britain
by Amazon.co.uk, Ltd.,
Marston Gate.